Table of Contents

Next Generation Series: Book 1
Sweet Crazy
Love
Yvonne Sibanda

Prologue

ELSIE COOPER stared intently at her book as everything else faded away into oblivion and it was just her and the difficult question. Slowly reading it while moving her lips but not making a sound, she was satisfied on the fact that she now understood what was being asked hence drew her calculator to her side, punched in a couple of numbers before punching in the equal sign and got the same answer.

She stared at it, scratched her head and uncrossed her legs under the table. She could swear she could hear her heart beating faster and her breathing grow heavy. This is so difficult, she thought before finally scribbling in the answer with a hope that her tutor wouldn't think she was guessing out everything like before.

To the onlooker she seemed to be paying full attention to the question as she usually did with everything else, taking her time and making sure that she had made the right decision or answered the question correctly.

Those deep brown eyes, the cute lips that were pursed in concentration said it all; she was on a mission to conquer the question even if it vexed her. Finally handing her tutor the notebook, Randy asked, "Is that your final answer?"

A flicker of uncertainty crossed her face before she gave a sharp nod and her lips slightly curled.

"How much do you think I should award you for your guess work?"

She huffed and Randy chuckled at her miffed expression.

He could tell that she had guessed out the answer and didn't follow what he had instructed her. Even though she had the calculator in hand, once a person punched in the wrong numbers they would always get the wrong answer out.

He sighed before commenting, "Old habits die hard I see." Taking the book from her hand, he advised "Relax love, Mathematics is not that hard as you think," before reaching out to the practice examination paper on the table and reading the question aloud.

They were settled outside Elsie's family home at the front porch while Randy tutored her in Mathematics. How she hated the subject but had to pass it since she had flunked it before. She had pushed it aside for long enough and now with her impending finals and if she intended to proceed further with her education; it was a must for her to have a pass of the damned subject.

Groaning in irritation and scratching her head, she thought, of course Randy would be quick to point out that it is not hard, he is a brainiac.

"Let me explain again so that you get it."

Randy smiled revealing a cute dimple on his left cheek that had her almost drooling and forgetting about Mathematics. She had a boyfriend and she should never forget that. The old Elsie who found her validation in men was gone, though being on the wild side still appealed to her minus of course having to deal with the consequences and emotional trauma.

She was Luc's daughter after all, the rebellious daughter who had taken after her father more than her mother's sweet, kind and faithful nature.

Randy motioned to the question before breaking down the formula used to solve it, detail by detail and finally she got it. The guy was good and to think she had been struggling a minute ago.

"Okay now I understand," she giggled and watched him roll his eyes.

"Thanks Randy for being patient with me," she added after she completed the rest of the questions without a hitch. She now knew if the questions happened to come in that manner she would ace them.

"No problem I am always happy to help. The problem is that you are lazy and don't want to take time to do this. You can ace this if you wanted to, you know that right?"

Elsie rolled her eyes, as if that's true, she thought.

"I am serious Elsie, how come you are able to do the other subjects perfectly and manage to get high marks, but when it comes to this one you suddenly develop an attitude?"

"Maybe it's because for every wrong answer the sound of a rod and the sting of it reaches my palms."

Randy chuckled at her answer. Learning at a public school especially in their hood was a challenge. The teachers at the public schools were used to dealing with rebellious, undisciplined, naughty students who started getting arrested from as early as twelve years. Hence they believed that they could beat not only discipline and good conduct into them but intelligence also.

Elsie's case and plight worsened since she wasn't that and had formerly learnt at a private school where a teacher wouldn't lump a student under one brand but would take time to know them and their weaknesses before finding a solution to their problem.

That was rather impossible in their kind of schools where one teacher had to teach over sixty students hence one of the causes why Elsie easily gave up and didn't try when she failed at her first attempt.

Another question again that had plagued him, why was she at public school and a girls one to top it all?

He shrugged off the thought and took a sip of orange juice before he answered, "I had forgotten you were a princess. Rita hates the rod also and she has been receiving that from kindergarten."

Elsie laughed. If they were another person who used to run from the line up when their teacher was gifting them with a beating, it was her best friend Rita.

She would be whimpering and muttering below her breath before the teacher even raised his hand with the rod. Everyone would start laughing and at times the teacher would laugh and let her go.

She was a teacher's pet, naturally intelligent and loved school. The only time she had to get paddled by the teacher was when the whole class had been caught making noise.

"Can we get back to our questions," Randy asked and received a nod before they delved back deep into the subject until they were interrupted by her mother's question while she stood at the door, "Hey, are you going to be doing statistics for the whole day?"

Elsie looked up and wondered for how long her mother had been standing there for. Taking a glimpse at her wrist watch she realized she and Randy had been doing Mathematics for over three hours.

"Gosh, I didn't realize that much time had gone," she remarked standing up from her chair and stretching her body. She could feel the tension ebb out from her body while she stretched and watched Randy greet her mother who had moved to the table and was looking at what they had been doing.

"I remember I struggled with Mathematics also, it was never my favorite subject" she stated with a grimace pasted on her face and Elsie giggled before she motioned with her arms, having caught her mom for being the quick one to judge. "But you are quick to point out that I play a lot that's why I flunked it." Her mother winked at her and replied with flourish, "At least I passed it on my first attempt and when I say you like playing, I mean it. You should cut back on sports and give it more attention."

Elsie rolled her eyes, "Geez mom, thanks for the confidence boost." Turning to Randy who was now packing up their stuff, she advised, "I will be back in a sec," before she dashed into the house.

She could hear their voices drift into the house as her mother asked Randy about his Nan and siblings. She swiftly picked up the small nicely wrapped gift she had left on her bed before her lesson and went back outside to the porch.

"Mom, let me see him out" she said and watched Randy pick up his backpack before he said his farewell to her mother and they slowly walked to the gate.

"I am glad my coursework is perfect because of you, thanks a lot."

Randy grinned and nodded.

That smile again, what was wrong with her and suddenly going all warm and fuzzy on Randy. She had known him for a long time to top it all and he was more like a brother to her.

Now that was a lie, since lately she had been noticing his tautly stretched shirt on his body, his tall frame reminding her of her uncle Greg and that dimple.

She wondered if he had a girlfriend. It was rather obvious he had one and a twinge of jealousy settled in the pit of her stomach at that thought. Clearing her throat she said, "I also have something for you. Rita told me it was your birthday last week, why didn't you mention." She stared accusingly at him while he shrugged his shoulders before answering, "We don't celebrate birthdays in our family."

"You don't mean it right," she stared at him, horrified. It was official, if Randy's family didn't, then she would make sure he did with her. She produced the small gift with flourish and handed it to him. She could see he was about to deny it but stopped him.

"Happy belated birthday and no am not going to take it back."

He sighed and opened it before he looked up again in surprise.

"What!! Don't you like it?"

She had bought one of the latest trending smart watches since she knew that he loved to jog a lot and keep fit. She instantly thought about him when she ordered it. The watch had a good navigation system which included a map complete with street names, music that he could factor into while running and of course the never ending battery. "I can't take this, this watch is pricey" he whispered and handed her the box. Elsie shook her head and frowned, "Yes you can. It's a birthday gift. You can also count it as payment since you don't want to charge for the extra lessons you have been giving me."

Finally Randy nodded to her relief and put it on. She had feared he wouldn't accept it.

"Thanks Elsie" he said touched by the gesture and hugged her.

"I will remember next time to get a cheap gift for you," she giggled, snuggling up to the embrace, enjoying the feel of his warm arms around her and wishing it would not end.

She wondered if being in his company for such a long time ever since he started tutoring her was the cause of the change in how she saw him.

She swallowed and took a few breaths hoping her breathing hadn't turned shallow and he could hear it.

Randy pulled away and looked at her with a raised brow before he said, "I have to go. All the best in your exam on Monday."

"Thanks a lot Randy for the help, I will surely pass. Will I get to see you again?"

"You know where to find me princess," he winked before getting into his car and driving off. Randy must have guessed that she was into him and he certainly didn't look fazed by it; oh boy, she thought and walked back to the house.

━━━◆━━━

"SO HOW DID THE LESSON go?" Rita her best friend asked her before she took a bite of the pizza. They were having a sleepover at Rita's house as usual after her mother forcibly told her to go and not try to be her parent with her new found concern.

"It was great, Randy explained everything perfectly. I think I will make it and already my coursework is great, I just need to push to get a B."

Rita rolled her eyes at that before remarking, "You do know you can get an A if you put much effort in Mathematics than give it attitude."

Elsie took a lunch bar from the food stuffs on the bed, unwrapped it before taking a bite. "Maybe" she answered thinking about what her mother and Randy had said. "It's just that am not a genius like you and Randy."

Rita was a natural. She caught on fast; she didn't need to study like her till it sunk in. While the teacher explained, she would instantly understand. Her friend chuckled and threw a pillow at her that she swiftly caught and put back on the bed. Taking a sip of the cola with a drinking straw, she continued, "Am serious. If it wasn't for my family having everything, I don't know what I will be doing."

"Designing duh" Rita scoffed.

Elsie chuckled "All because of my mom and Uncle Ethan."

Somehow amidst getting most of her father's vices she also had her mother's talent in designing. Already her life was paved out and it totally had nothing to do with Mathematics. She intended to be a fashion designer. Come to think of it Nita already knew what she wanted and Wendy also.

"Speaking about Uncle Ethan, do you think he will be fine?"

Elsie nodded her head as she was hoping for the best. It had been a month after uncle Ethan had woken up from his comma. Her mother explained it to her that he had suffered some kind of memory loss hence wouldn't be the same Ethan that she knew. Well she wasn't going to allow him to forget her and her young sisters that fast and she had put it upon herself to remind him.

She made sure she visited him all the time at uncle Greg's place and they had gone out for a couple of dates.

It was funny though since he still was the same adult, always chiding her to behave and be a good girl. The man definitely didn't have a fun bone in his body.

"At least he still remembers how to splurge money on treats," she commented with a laugh, since he was the one who had bought the food they were eating at the moment. She had called him and asked him to buy a box of pizza, some fries, chicken, candy and sodas for her sleepover with Rita.

Rita was alone at home, her brothers having gone camping with her mom's boyfriend while her mother had travelled out of town because of work and would be returning the next day.

Elsie bit into the spicy chicken thigh and groaned. Uncle Ethan had been surprised at the order not believing that the food was just for two teenagers, girls to top it all. Where they not on diet to look trim and svelte, had been his question when she was spelling out the order.

"I almost didn't come for the sleepover today. Mom is the one who told me to not break the tradition; she preferred being alone and not having me checking up on her all the time." She rolled her eyes at that. Rita took a bite of the Hawaiian pizza in her hand before she asked, "How would you feel if your mom was to get married to Ethan though?"

Elsie giggled before replying, "I would finally have my perfect family. Uncle Ethan has been there for me ever since I can remember. Even in those moments when I wished my dad was there, uncle Ethan took that role, like the time he held my hand while I was in hospital for a checkup, scared to death and he was there muttering that it will be fine?"

"When was that? You never told me about it?"

Elsie bit her tongue. She didn't want to talk about the past and here she had been about to blurt it out. If Rita knew that side about her, she might not be willing to be her friend.

She asked instead, "How about you, how do you feel about your mother being in a relationship."

Rita frowned and took a bite from the pizza while her mind went on overdrive as she thought on how to answer Elsie.

Her mother had recently started dating and she didn't know how to take the whole thing about having a new man in the family. Drew and Barry liked him and with this camping trip they had taken together, they would definitely be defending the man afterwards.

She missed her dad so much. He had been sick for a while and she had hoped he would get better. That never happened and now she didn't have him in her life.

She finally answered after a long pause, "I don't know. I just thought it was too early. My dad has been gone for four months and then we are introduced to this stranger and his irritating son and mom says hey am dating, it's all so confusing."

Elsie giggled at that. Then she thought her family was the weird one.

They continued having their meal in harmonious silence and cleared the things on the bed afterwards. Rita lay back on the bed and Elsie remained sitting cross legged on it. Her mind had wandered off to the events of the afternoon. She was rather curious hence she braved it and asked, hoping at the same time that Rita would not read much into her question.

"Does Randy have a girlfriend?"

The question got Rita propping up her head against her hand and looking at her with a raised brow.

"What!! I am just curious, that's all" she blurted out. Like she had thought, her friend read too much into her statement than she intended to reveal.

Finally Rita replied, "From what I can tell, he doesn't, why do you ask, are you maybe in looove with him?"

Elsie squealed and threw a pillow at her friend who swiftly avoided it.

"Is it possible to like two guys at the same time?" she probed further and chuckled at Rita's surprised face. She hoped she wouldn't think the worst about her, yet that's what she was feeling at the moment.

"I think it is possible to like two guys at the same time, but you will have to settle for one at the end, than string them both along. What they deserve is to find someone who would love them whole heartedly not sharing the love between two or three or four."

She was making funny shocked expressions as she added the numbers by flipping the fingers while Elsie laughed. Rita should have chosen being a psychologist as her career not what she intended to do, she thought.

"I hear you doctor Rita Duncan, loud and clear." Elsie saluted her before she asked, "What about you, don't you want to date?"

Rita scoffed, "My mom advised that I date when I am done with school and working and as for you thinking about Randy in those terms you are being silly, Randy is not your type."

The dismissive way Rita said it made her open her mouth and shut it again without commenting. She finally asked after a short pause, "And what is my type pray tell me Rita?"

"Don't you have a boyfriend? Sean. Remember him, the tall, cute guy who only wears suits reminding us of boss baby. Now that is your type. He is sophisticated, has a good job, comes from a good and influential background and he is loaded. By the way does Sean even have a pair of jeans in his closet?" Rita asked with a slight twitch on her mouth.

"So are you saying Randy doesn't fit into that category?" Elsie asked with a frown on her face while her friend rolled her eyes before she replied, "Yes. Randy will not be able to give you the life style you are used to."

"I don't know about that," Elsie said and decided to lie back on the bed. "I mean.... I love Sean and on paper he has everything that you mentioned but I wonder if I can have the passionate kind of love that would make me go crazy and lose it with him."

"Ooh like the one you see in movies and you think Randy can give you that. Which Randy are you talking about? The quiet, unassuming guy who happens to live next door, are you for real? The one who terms us as the silly twittering girls and treats us like his young sisters and who barely has noticed that you have boobs? I wonder where do you get passion in all that mix."

Elsie giggled at Rita's summation of the whole thing; of course Rita will always see him as their older brother than anything else.

Blame it on the tutoring sessions but she was attracted to him and there she had been thinking Rita will just stop at the fact that it was fine for her to like two guys.

"Yes our big brother Randy" she drawled.

Rita sat up on the bed and clutched at a pillow before she asked, "Ook let's say hypothetically you happened to leave Daddy Sean.."

Elsie rolled her eyes at that since Rita always claimed Sean acted more mature to the point he qualified to be in their parents' age group. The guy was just four years older than them while Randy was five years older.

Randy had recently completed college as a Mechanic and was working different jobs including being her Mathematics tutor while Sean would be completing his Law degree in a few months times.

"And dated Randy..." Rita was saying. She attentively listened. "As you can see Sean has the fat bank account, he comes from your world, he is about to become a lawyer once he is done with varsity, not to forget he is good on the eye. Then we have Randy, he has responsibilities, his young brother, sister and his nana. He is in-between jobs not at all what your mom might recommend it terms of 'stability'. With Randy you will have to give up your lifestyle, you will join us including under the tree in order to get your hair plaited and bargain your way in everything."

"Geez when did you become this mature and start thinking in those lines" Elsie asked after giving it a thought.

"Am just pointing out the facts on why I said that he is not your type and don't say it..."

Elsie had opened her mouth to protest.

"Randy is not the type to accept help from a woman and you know that. He will not get your money even if he knew your bank balance was fat."

"That's being too proud, I mean hypothetically speaking."

Rita would say that about Randy since she also had refused her assistance when Elsie tried to help her out with her tuition for Medical school.

"It's self-respect, call it pride but it's our dignity being put on the line. This side of town we work for everything that we have."

"We do the same also," Elsie pouted her lips.

"Did you work for the money you wanted to offer me for my education?"

"Well that would be coming..."

Rita interrupted her again by raising her hand. "That's what I meant, your trust fund. We don't have that. After Randy's parents passed he had to leave school and do odd jobs so he could save for college. Can you do that, give up on your dreams and pursue something else to make ends meet. His nana's pension isn't much so he carries the bulk in taking care of Lilly and Raff; his life is not an easy one. Can you manage with all that?"

Rita looked distant as she said that before she shrugged and continued, "I don't know Else, maybe you can manage our lifestyle, at the end it's your decision, but don't string both guys along that's all I am saying. Either you are with Sean and fully content with him or you leave him to be with Randy, giving Sean the chance to be with someone else who will love and cherish him."

Elsie huffed; her friend was acting as if she had two boyfriends when she just had Sean her official boyfriend and Randy her friend. She had been curious that's why she had asked. She somehow felt guilty for the fact that her family was well off, especially after hearing Rita talk. What did they worry about actually apart from, which country they would visit over the holidays or the brand on their clothes if it was a designer or a knockoff? She cleared her throat and Rita yawned.

"I am surely going to miss these sleepover talks once we are at uni."

"Same here" Rita said and yawned again. She lay back on the bed since they had both sat up again amidst their talk and whispered "Goodnight, feeling sleepy."

Elsie stiffly nodded before she lay back also but couldn't sleep like Rita who easily dozed off into dreamland.

She was thinking on what they had spoken about. Rita was right, would she manage with Randy if it meant she had to leave everything behind. What about Randy, would he fit in with her people. Her family was friendly enough but the circle of friends around them could be termed more on the vain side than anything else.

With their barbed remarks on anything that was beneath them. Sean had scowled a bit the first time she asked him to drop her by Rita's place, as if he didn't want to be there at all. He had been dressed in his tailor made suit, a stark contrast against the background while Rita had rolled her eyes at him.

She had whispered afterwards that she thought Sean was prideful and had an ego that needed to be deflated before they tied the knot in future.

She knew Sean was a good person; it was just that it had been the first time for him to venture to the other side of town and it might have taken him by surprise that she had friends from there.

Randy and Sean might have the common trait of being committed at whatever they did, yet she doubted they would be the best of friends. One wore jeans and worked with his hands, fixing cars for a living while another wore suits all the time and was being groomed to take over the family law firm one day.

She couldn't even imagine Sean being laid back and getting his hands dirty not even in her wildest dreams.

Randy will end up looking like a sore thumb among them and might eventually resent her.

It's not like her family were super rich like Bill Gates but they had enough. The only reason why she even became used to Rita was because her mother sent her to public school as a punishment from her many misdeeds while her sisters still went to the expensive boarding school out of town.

Was she beginning to think differently because of that, being around people who didn't have much but had what counted, like a happy family?

Ever since she could remember she had always longed for that. Her home was a chaotic one with both parents living under the same roof but separated. Sean's was the same.

She worried her lip. Maybe that's how it was meant to be. No one ever got everything that they wanted.

Randy's parents passed when he was nineteen and he stayed with his nana, young sister and brother. From the framed photos she had seen on the wall, their family had been a happy one. Complete. It still had that warmth because of his nana who made sure that all the children stayed inline.

The old woman laughed a lot and had a lot of laugh lines as proof of that. Elsie had instantly liked her the moment Rita introduced her. Randy was a model grandson, student, brother and friend. She rather envied both Randy and Rita. Though they might teasingly call her a princess who had everything, she at times felt they had more than she could ever have.

She heaved a sigh and decided to shut her eyes. What was the use of thinking in such terms? She was with Sean and they had already planned their future together, and like Rita had mentioned Randy didn't notice she even had boobs. To him she would always be like his young sister.

Chapter One

1 year and 9 months later.

"FUNKY HAIRSTYLE check, make up perfect, check, backpack set with the things that I will need check, over the top clothes to show that I am a fashion student" Elsie turned around and looked into the full length mirror before stating , "check. IPhone check, bluetooth headset, check. Guess I am set and ready for my long awaited second semester at varsity, that's a double check."

Elsie smiled at her reflection in the mirror; fully conscious at the fact that she looked great while muttering under her breath after seeing to it that everything she needed was in order.

Picking up her bag and car keys, she rushed to the kitchen to have her breakfast before school.

"Morning princess," her step dad Ethan Ross greeted while holding her squealing young brother Eric in his arms. He whistled when he took note on what she was wearing. Before he could comment, Lorraine and Laura rushed into the kitchen noisy as ever managing to make Elsie roll her eyes.

"I don't know how you manage all this, I can't wait to leave this house," Elsie commented.

"Young missy, the only time you will leave from under this roof is when you are safely in your husband's house," her mother spoke as she got into the kitchen.

Ethan gave up the fight and placed Eric on the ground. He watched in dismay as Eric crawled off as fast as his tiny knees and hands could carry him trailing behind the twins before he straightened and leaned towards his beautiful wife for a kiss.

"Morning," he whispered.

"Ugh get a room," Elsie said loudly enough for her parents to hear and watched her mother turn around to face her and place her hands on her waist.

"Ugh to you too as if you don't kiss with Sean."

Elsie dramatically closed her ears while her mother chuckled. "I mean it Else, marriage first and you leave home. No daughter of mine will stay alone in an apartment, who knows what you will be up to."

"Daaad."

Elsie looked to Ethan pleadingly who shrugged his shoulders and said, "I should check on the children and see what they are up to."

"Cowaaard," she giggled at his retreating back. Her step dad was more of the peace kind of loving person and usually retreated before things got out of hand. When he set his foot down though, his word was final and the law of the house.

At the moment he appeared to be in agreement with his wife on the fact that Elsie would be driving to and from varsity.

He had even stated that she give him 1001 reasons on why she wanted to move out.

"Are we that much of a nuisance that you want to leave us love?" her mother asked with a furrowed brow pasted on her face.

"It's not that ma and you know it. I am twenty, am at varsity and an adult. Most adults actually get excited over the fact that their children are moving out. They celebrate over the free room and turn it into a storage room or game room."

"Well we are not most parents," her mother quipped back before turning back to the stove to prepare breakfast for everyone. Elsie heaved a heavy sigh and dropped the matter. What was the use since it was rather a long ongoing argument that she was failing to win.

"Ok, ok, I give up. I will not move out. I will stay with you till the day I diiiee. No marriage for me since I have such loving parents," she drawled, waving her arms in defeat. Her mother chuckled, "Ooh now I get it, you want some action and we are getting in your way."

"Ugh maaa," Elsie shook her head and decided to put her energies into buttering a slice of toast instead.

"Speaking about action, so are you wearing that on your first day to school?"

"Yes, is it bad? I thought I looked great."

"It's a creative outfit; great buut does Sean like it when you dress like that?"

Elsie rolled her eyes. "Sean is rather being stuffy and controlling all of a sudden."

She knew that as their ten year plan they had agreed that they would get married once she graduated from varsity but that didn't necessarily mean that he was meant to start controlling her now before they had even tied the knot.

Her mother shrugged, "You chose him, I didn't so stop looking at me with accusation in your eyes," she advised before calling out to her brood and husband that breakfast was ready.

"And that's my cue to leave," Elsie said and stood up from the kitchen stool before she hugged her mother and waved to the rest of the family members who came rushing into the kitchen.

The way her chaotic family acted as if it was world war III was one of the reasons she didn't always bring her friends over.

Her parents were just something else as they tended to interrogate whoever managed to knock on the door looking for her and pointing out that Elsie already had a boyfriend, who she was meant to get married to in a few years' time, ugh. Everything was set. Her future was bright and they were not going to allow anyone to take her away from her plans.

She regretted telling her step dad in confidence about them. At the time, he had stated that he was proud of her for thinking ahead about her future and her relationship with Sean.

The minor setback is that, he told her mother, who spoke to Mrs. Grace Compton, Sean's mom, who told her husband and both families started acting like one unit.

Everyone was just bent on ruining her life and there was no way of escaping her relationship, not that she wanted to but still. She didn't intend to be scandalous like them as their scandals made her wish she could crawl into a pit and never come out.

Already photos of her dad and Abby were plastered on billboards, the Abby who had once tried to ruin her mom's life while her mother had her young handsome husband on her end.

How she so missed Nita and Wendy who appeared to be the quiet and scandal free ones in the family.

Getting into her car she drove off, leaving her chaotic family behind for just a few hours. She wondered what Rita was up to and took note in her mind to give her a call in the evening. She must have settled well at Medical school and doing what she was good at, researching.

Her car made a funny sound out of the ordinary and she decided to turn to the nearest garage before she travelled further. Though she had another car in the garage, she appeared not to be able to part away with her cute mini cooper. They had so much history together. She sighed loudly as she drove after taking note it was safe to make a turn.

The funny sound happened again and she was relieved that she had reached the garage when the car went dead.

The garage had a few cars in it and she couldn't spot any mechanics from where she was. Stepping out from the car, she motioned to the lady who was seated behind a desk. "Halloo, need a bit of help here, my car." The lady yelled to one of the mechanics while Elsie rolled her eyes, geez did she have to screech like that. She got back into the car and waited.

"Hi" a deep voice that she couldn't easily forget drifted through. The last time she had met him had been before her final exams at high school, when she decided to stay away because of her sudden crush.

"Randy," she screamed and got out of the car before hugging him.

"Hey Elsie," he chuckled returning the hug before stating, "I am a bit dirty if you didn't notice."

"Ooh you," she muttered and punched his arm before stepping away.

"How have you been? It's been long, how is nana, Lilly and Raff?" she asked and Randy raised his hands. "Whoa princess, nothing changes there, you still chatter so much like a bird."

She huffed.

"Tell me what's the problem with the car and I will answer your questions while I attend to it."

"I don't know, it made some funny sounds before it went dead completely." He nodded and went back to take his tool box before he came back.

He was still the same, with the attractive body that had made her almost drool and at the moment he was spotting a shadow of a beard and moustache. He had removed the work suit jacket and tied it around his waist and had a grey t-shirt that was tautly stretched over his abs. She could swear that side about him had become broader.

He popped open the hood and began taking a look at it while he told her that nana and his little brother and sister were fine before asking her about her family.

Randy chuckled and kept on nodding as she chatted on about her mom getting married; having Eric and now Eric was a nuisance to her things as everything belonged in his tiny mouth.

"It has been long indeed since we last met."

"Being under lockdown makes people miss out on a lot of things," she replied with a grimace and he nodded. They were still recovering from the corona virus that had taken the world and everyone by surprise including changing their way of doing things.

That had also made a dent into her ten year plan since she delayed in going to uni because of it and marriage would only come after she was done. Though it was still there, the rules had been loosened a bit and people were able to go back to work and regain some semblance of normalcy back in their lives. They had managed to create an effective vaccine and the virus had become just as common as the flue.

"You can start the engine now," he advised and she turned on the key. The car purred to life and she sighed relieved.

"Thank you, thank you so much Randy," she said and asked, "Where do I pay up?"

He shook his head, "No need, it was nothing much that I had to do."

"We should meet up for a drink Randy, I can still get you on your same digits right."

He nodded and watched her drive off. Tyler was walking his way when he carried the tool box back to the other cars he had been checking out before the interruption.

"Who was that cute little thing?" Tyler asked with a wink. Randy frowned. "A friend."

"His girlfriend," Jolene at the front desk shouted. "And a rich one, look at that" she flipped to the center page of the magazine that had a poster of Elsie. "It reads she is the next generation of a breed of designers in the making.

Tyler whistled, "If she is that, why didn't she pay?"

He scowled and Randy told him to take it off his pay check and stop being on his case.

His boss cum friend advised, "Don't forget and lose your head over her, she is not in your league."

As if, Randy rolled his eyes at that notion. Elsie had always been like a young sister to him and nothing more. Having met her in her sophomore year at high school because she was Rita's new friend from the suburbs he didn't pay that much attention to her.

Rita and Elsie were sort of like a nuisance in his life as they would come over for chats with his nana and evade his privacy in his room.

The silly twittering girls, he had called them while his young brother and sister enjoyed their company.

He chuckled; Elsie was still an innocent and not at all what he would fall for.

Chapter Two

RANDY CHUCKLED at the thought of Elsie's talkative nature as he got into the house after work. His nana was settled on the recliner in the living room, sewing a scarf as she usually did. "Hey Nan," he greeted and kissed her on the forehead.

"Randy how was your day?" she asked and he replied.

"Are Raff and Lilly back from school?"

His nana shook her head and continued knitting before she said, "They had sports today after their lessons."

Raff and Lilly were twins and his young brother and sister. He loved them to bits and at the age of fifteen they always managed to give him grief at times. He smothered a laugh at the fact that when he thought of them, he thought of another girl who had literally hurled herself at him when she saw him.

"Guess who came by the garage today though it was to get her car fixed."

His grandmother looked at him and shrugged her shoulders. He exhaled noisily; Nan at times could act all strict when she was actually one of the coolest grannies. He could see the frown starting to appear on her forehead and hoped she would not start with the whole marriage stuff.

The moment he hit twenty five it seemed to have signaled to her that he had to settle down.

"Elsie," he said. Her face lit up as expected and she asked, "How is she, its time she paid me a visit, it has been long since I met that pretty kind young lady."

He resisted the urge to roll his eyes at the emphasis she was making on pretty and kind.

"She is great, still the same chatter box."

"She must be of marriageable age now," his grandmother said and he chuckled. Now she wanted to throw Elsie at him.

"Nan she is still young and has a lot of dreams to fulfill before she settles down."

His grandmother scoffed, "Just go and wash up boy before you ask for a hiding. I don't know what is wrong with your generation; you delay in everything and hope that all goes well after you have messed up during the delaying phase. Like I said, I don't want a girl turning up pregnant outside my home" she grumbled and Randy laughed.

He decided to excuse himself before the old lady had high blood pressure because of him. He needed a bath, food and rest before he went to his other job. He certainly didn't have time to shop around for a woman.

⬥

ELSIE'S DAY AFTER THE garage incident was full of activity as she went from lecture to lecture and forgot about her crush. It was when she was driving back home that she decided to give Sean a call. As usual, Sean couldn't take her out on a date because he was busy with work.

"Will you ever have time for me?" she sulked and could hear him laugh. "What has gotten into you all of a sudden? I thought you like the whole giving each other space thing. How did you put it, the heart grows fonder when your loved one is away?"

"I know what I had said Sean, but can I at least get an hour of your company."

Sean sighed and asked, "What is going on love."

Elsie bit her tongue and could clearly imagine him sitting back on his chair about to interrogate her. She knew the cause of her unease, meeting Randy again after such a long time. She thought she had her crush under control but she had been wrong.

"Nothing, don't you want to meet with me?"

"Tell you what, I have a business dinner in the evening, will you please be my plus one. I will pick you up at seven."

She huffed, "You know I hate that boring stuff, but I am game since you asked so politely." Sean laughed before he told her he loved her craziness and hung up. With that done, she now contemplated on what to wear. She decided to drop by her mom's boutique and grab an outfit for the formal affairs that Sean always attended. Already she dreaded meeting some of the ladies who appeared to want to cling to her boyfriend. He was a catch after all, and this dinner would for a while take her mind from straying to unchartered waters.

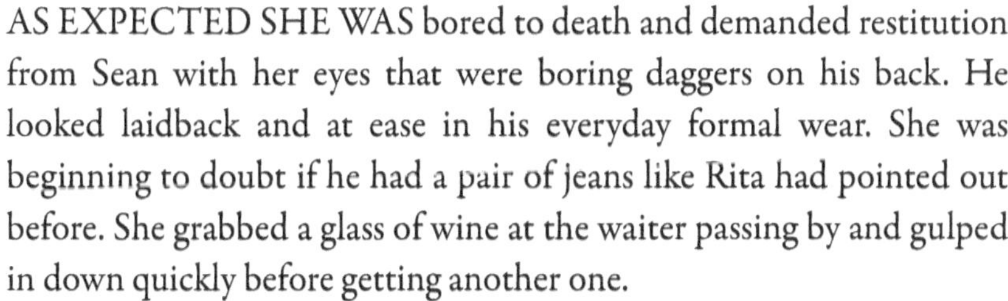

AS EXPECTED SHE WAS bored to death and demanded restitution from Sean with her eyes that were boring daggers on his back. He looked laidback and at ease in his everyday formal wear. She was beginning to doubt if he had a pair of jeans like Rita had pointed out before. She grabbed a glass of wine at the waiter passing by and gulped in down quickly before getting another one.

"Elsie," a familiar voice addressed her. As usual Shirley was scantily dressed and having a lot of makeup that could be contained in a quarter part of her mom's cosmetic department. What caught her eye the most though were the big hooters over her chest, Shirley had normal sized boobs before?

"I see you are spotting on some new release there," she said, sarcasm dripping from her tongue. The woman didn't notice at all but rather smiled and replied, "You like them? It's been two months since I had the surgery."

She really needed to escape, but the lady followed her when she moved for another wine glass. "Don't you think you are drinking a lot today, I mean you have been on the bender before and we wouldn't want that to happen again." A raised brow was targeted on the wine glass she was holding. "I have it under control Shirley and there is no need for you to worry about me," she snorted back. Shirley was Justin's big sister, the Justin that she made a lot of mistakes with in the name of love. Shirley was just a year older to Justin and seemed to love to goad her over her past misdeeds. "It has been seven years now so that's rather old to be bringing up my lapse in judgment."

"Well you might say seven but I heard all those years can be lost in an instant," Shirley flicked her fingers for emphasis. "Sooo slow down on the booze" she finished with a fake smile pasted on her face.

"By the way did you see Justin, he is here."

That had Elsie reaching out for another glass. For a second she had managed to forget about her past but her subconscious wasn't letting her this time, since this was the day she always dreaded the most every year.

The pain of it had slowly faded but the impact seemed to still linger at the recess of her mind, and with Shirley mentioning Justin, she doubted she would survive.

A hand touched her shoulder, startling her as she turned and sighed in relief when she realized it was Sean.

"Hey love." He swiftly took away the glass and she wanted to protest. "I think you have had enough for the day." He whispered in her ear and nodded to Shirley before walking away with her towards the door.

Once they were outside he asked, "What has gotten into you Elsie?"

Let's see, naughty thoughts she was having about Randy, meeting infuriating Shirley and being told her once upon a time lover boy was at the function also.

"Nothing was just having fun," she feigned a frown and failed dismally. She could feel that the wine had loosened her up a bit and she was no longer nervous. She could do it, brave her meeting with Justin as she usually did. While he stared at her with that knowing glimmer in his eyes, and a slight curl on his lips as he happened to know her in more ways than she could ever have wished.

Gulping in a few breaths of the cool fresh air, she glanced at Sean who was leading her away from the building to the car, she knew they weren't any hopes of going back to that party seeing how determined he was. Sean knew how out of control she could be and had swiftly left with her before she caused havoc. "Since we attended your stuffy dinners why don't we pass by a club also?"

"I have work tomorrow and you have school."

"You know what Sean," she stopped and turned to face him before poking his broad chest, "You don't have a fun bone in your body. All you think about is work, work and more work. Do you even find me desirable or when you look at me, am just a case study for you to do."

She was toying with his tie and Sean grabbed her hand.

"You are drunk," he muttered.

"I am drunk in my love for you." She pulled his head by the tie and kissed him. Sean pulled away, "No Elsie not like this." She scoffed, for a Compton he surely acted uppity tight; she turned away from him and resumed walking to the car.

He had to keep her in the seat throughout the drive as she would poke her head and start yelling.

By the time they got home, she had calmed down and was softly snoring away, having dozed off. The only times she ever got this way was when... his mind came to a dead still. Why had he been so insensitive? He had totally forgotten the date since he had been busy with work. This was the day when she had the accident and almost died.

He had met people who appeared to have overcome the guilt but on this day Elsie seemed to relieve it somehow as it surfaced back. He got off the car and moved to the passenger door before he helped her out of the car and carried her to the door. Her mother opened it and let him in before he walked towards her room.

He greeted her after placing her on the bed. "That bad huh," her mother asked. "I had forgotten about it and it just clicked when we were coming back."

"She was happy in the morning and I thought she had forgotten" her mother replied. "Thanks Sean for bringing her safe and sound. She is lucky to have you in her life."

"It's no bother Mrs. Ross I care about her," he whispered and walked out of Elsie's room.

Aggy watched Sean leave the house before she shut the door after him and went back to bed. Ethan had finished changing Eric's diaper and was rubbing his belly as he dosed off. "How did it go?" he asked.

"Same as always, you know when you have that hope that it will not happen again and then subconsciously she remembers."

He tucked Eric in before walking to his bed. "She will be fine; I mean seven years is a long time."

Aggy shook her head and scoffed, "You don't know Elsie, and she will keep beating herself over it till the day she dies. It's like that insurance advert with those monsters. It grows and bursts and starts growing again for the next year."

Ethan smiled at that analogue before he pulled his wife into his arms and tenderly kissed her. "Let's be grateful for today that the incidence has passed until next year then" he said before he shut his eyes and dozed off.

⸻⬤⸻

ELSIE WOKE UP WITH a pounding headache and a vibrating phone the next day in the morning. Her mother had placed a packet of aspirin and a glass of water on the side of the bed. She reached out to it, popped one pill and gulped down the water before she answered the phone. It was her uncle Garret. "Hey love, your mom informed me that you had travelled down memory lane yesterday," he said after she greeted him.

"It's one of those things Pastor G," she answered and could hear him chuckle before he commented, "How many times have I spoken to you about self-condemnation. It's not good. Whatever happened in the past should stay there. It's no use beating yourself over it and you are not doing anything wrong by moving on with your life and living princess. You are receiving what God has given you by his grace and accepting that Christ paid it all with his precious blood."

She nodded before she realized that he wouldn't see that since they were speaking over the phone and answered back. She spoke with her uncle for a while before she hung up feeling a bit revived.

Her phone rang again, it was Sean this time. "I am so, so, sorry Sean for yesterday," was the first thing that came out of her mouth when she answered it.

"It's okay love, though am beginning to have second thoughts about having your crazy self in my family."

She giggled; he had been saying that over the years. "Are you fine though," he asked and his concern pulled at her heart. "Yes I am I promise it will not happen again."

She could actually imagine him roll back his eyes at that last statement. They chatted for a while before she hung up. Rushing to the bathroom after taking note of the time, she got ready for school.

Yesterday had been different somehow. She could swear she had forgotten about everything until she started berating herself over what she was feeling towards Randy.

The year of distancing herself from him proved to be of no use as she found herself back at square one. That's when it also seemed to come back. The bad decisions that she had managed to make over her life. Like her uncle had mentioned, self-condemnation sucked. It sent one into a deeper slump. She felt she was a bad girl and she couldn't be faithful to Sean.

She was her father's daughter. No matter how much she tried to tell herself that she wasn't him. Randy hadn't been the only one in the four years she had been with Sean. They had been other guys she had flirted with and Sean didn't mind, except with Randy it was different, he just couldn't be shrugged off like the others as if he were nothing and it was just pure fun.

One glass of wine became two and so on. God she was a mess, she thought. It will serve her right if handsome kind Sean left her for good. She didn't deserve anything good to come her way, she thought and sighed.

She stared at the mirror and her hair. Time she dyed it another color to mask the torment she felt in her heart. A bright shade of red would do, she thought and since her skin color boded on the lighter side, it would be perfect. With her mind made up she dressed up and left for the kitchen where the chaos in her home was in full swing.

Chapter Three

NANA WAS knitting the winter jerseys for the twins when she heard the sound of a car engine and wondered who it could be. Their hood didn't have that many people who drove. She leaned on the window and spotted a vibrant red color of hair emerging from the car and smiled. Elsie hadn't changed at all and still hid her feelings through her always colorful hair choices.

Moving to the door, she opened it before the young lady had reached her and stood akimbo.

"Well, well, look who decided to grace us with her presence today."

Elsie chuckled and waved off her remark with her hands before she hugged her.

"I missed you nana and wasn't expecting such a cold welcome."

Nan scoffed, "You call this cold when I rushed to the door and forgot about my aching bones." Elsie giggled and was ushered into the house by the old woman. "How have you been my dear child?" she asked.

"Great Nan, how about you and the family?"

"As you can see, they do not stop growing," Nan motioned to the jersey she was knitting. After the pleasantries had been shared she stood up to prepare tea for the young lady. She loved her and always thought Elsie and Randy would make a perfect match. Except her grandson was too blind to see and Elsie was convinced she was meant to be with Sean. She rolled her eyes at that. She didn't have anything against Sean Compton but she believed Elsie's personality clashed with his.

She could already see Sean trying to control a free spirit like Elsie.

"So how is Sean doing," Nan asked once she got back to the living room and placed the tray on the table. "They wasn't a need for all this nana," Elsie said and smiled when the old woman rolled her eyes. "Sean is great. Always busy with work."

"Hmmm, I expected him to have married you by now?"

Elsie choked on her tea before placing the cup back on the table. "After varsity, that was the agreement."

Nan nodded her head and resumed with her knitting. "I have been telling Randy to settle down. It's now time, don't you think." She smothered a laugh when she noticed Elsie tear at her bun but not eat it, so the young lady still fancied her grandson. "I guess it is time," Elsie finally said.

"Don't you have women that you would like to suggest?"

"Me?" Elsie looked incredulously at her, "I mean I wouldn't have an idea on the kind of woman that he would want. Randy once mentioned he wanted one more of his age."

"It's your duty to find that lady then." Nan said sternly before she winked. Randy came in as Elsie was trying to compose herself over nana's suggestion. "Afternoon nan," he greeted and kissed her on the forehead as he tended to do before he greeted Elsie and left for his room.

"Look at him, miserable as hell. All that he does is wake up, work and work till he drops. Can you believe he doesn't even have a girlfriend? I fear he will die a bachelor and a miserable one. What he needs is a woman who will remove him from that cocoon."

Elsie giggled. She knew Nan was exaggerating the matter and jesting. There was no way that Randy would be single. She decided to humor the old woman and announced. "We will get him hitched soon enough. I think they might be a few ladies that I can recommend; even Rita is bound to know a few also."

"That's settled then," Nan happily said. Randy was getting back into the living room when he heard the last words. "What's settled?" he asked and both ladies giggled. These two tended to act as thick as thieves and he wondered what they were up to now. He had a reprieve ever since the lockdown but now he guessed Elsie would be a constant visitor again to his home.

"Nothing, I had dropped by just to check on you all before I left for my afternoon lesson." She stood up from the couch. Nan followed suit. "This was a surprise indeed. I hope to see you again. Greetings to your parents" she said as she accompanied Elsie to her car. Nan whispered something to Elsie that had her roll her eyes. Their easy banter used to make Randy jealous but now he had decided to take it as that. After she had driven off Nan remarked. "Are you sure you are not ready to settle down."

"Where would I get the time and energy to invest in such a relationship?"

Nan rolled her eyes, "Elsie is available."

"Elsie has a boyfriend, she is young and did you see that hair." Nan laughed. She had said the same to Elsie when she was accompanying her to the car. If she wanted Randy to take her seriously she had to tone down.

⟶●⟵

ON THURSDAY NIGHT, two weeks after meeting nana after a long time Elsie called Sean and asked him to be her date for the annual fashion show at school. As usual he had other commitments. She was rather furious with him for not making time for their relationship and bluntly asked him if he wanted to be in this at all before she hung up. For how long would he drag her on like that? Since they were no lessons on Friday as everyone was getting ready, she decided to go to the salon and prepare also for the show. She wasn't going to stay mopping around in bed while the world moved on happily without her. If Sean wasn't interested then she would go with someone else. She made a call to Randy that went to his voice mail. He called later on when he was free and took her up on the offer, chuckling at the same time warning her that he didn't know a snitch about fashion.

"Make sure you dress in what you feel comfortable in. You know fashion is not about the brand, yes we have that, but if you can pull off a look, in no time you will be having people imitating that," she said cheerfully over the phone before she hung up. It was agreed, Randy would meet her at the campus and since she wasn't in the mood to drive, she would hire a taxi to take her there. She leaned back on the chair as her hairdresser giggled. "It seems you finally secured a date." Rolling her eyes she remarked, "Imagine. It's as if I have to kneel before one of the men can take me out."

"For such a beautiful girl like you, thought men would be lining up to date you."

"Ha, ha, not even. Maybe it's the hair." She turned to face her hairdresser before she said, "Change of plans. Today I am going el naturel," she giggled at the horrified expression of her hairdresser. "Serious."

"Yes, serious" she said and laid back on the chair and let her hair dresser do magic with her hair.

⸻ ◈ ⸻

RANDY WHISTLED AND heard Elsie giggle in return. She had toned down and it was rather taking him by surprise. Like his nana had mentioned, she surely had grown up. He berated himself for not having noticed before. Gone was the colorful hair to be replaced by shoulder length black hair. The glorious strands were beckoning for him to slide his fingers into then while her long simple pink dress clung to her body. It had a lacy bodice with nude laced sleeves and pooled at her feet. The fish tail skirt had a side slit reaching her thighs while the top part clung to her body accentuating her hips.

"You like" she asked and turned her foot clad in light pink high heeled shoes sideways, swaying her hips at the same time.

He coughed, he didn't like, he loved the look.

He cleared his throat and asked, "Shall we?" before offering her his arm and they walked to where the hall was situated on the campus.

Elsie had almost drooled when she saw Randy walking up to the cab. Then he said he didn't know a snitch of fashion. He was dressed in a white t-shirt and blue suede blazer with a dark blue shade on the lapels and patched arms along with blue ripped jeans. He was clean shaven and his hair cropped into a fashionable hairstyle. She hoped nana hadn't been the one who suggested the look. The old woman was relentless. She chuckled at the thought and allowed Randy to lead her on as they walked to the huge hall.

"Whoa" Randy remarked when they got in and he took in the fashionable clothes worn by the students, their friends, dates and families.

A guy in a printed shirt and shorts nodded at them and Randy smothered a laugh.

"You know he reminds me of the colorful and daring dresser Elsie" he commented still looking at the retreating back of the young man.

She giggled, "That short is pretty tight. His junk must be suffocating."

"You are a naughty young lady" he retorted, surprised that she would make such statements.

"I notice things also" she winked and led him on through the crowded masses. They received a program from one of the students standing at the beginning of the aisle before they moved in between the seats on the side and chose the ones that were closer to the aisle so they could view everything.

"This feels like those actual fashion shows on t.v." he commented after they had settled down. She almost rolled her eyes at that statement.

"I had forgotten you are a virgin in this kind of setting."

Randy laughed and reached out to her hand, leaning in so she could hear him above the people talking, "I am not interested in such things my princess." He smelt good and with the way he was looking at her she blushed. Nan had been right after all. Wait until she told Rita that Randy now noticed that she had boobs and wasn't a boy.

"Nan was indeed right. You do need a woman to start living and very fast" she goaded in jest.

"Ha ha smarty pants; I will not let you drag me down that path. Nan tried and now she sends you to do her dirty work."

"It was worth a try," she giggled and settled back on the chair after noticing that everyone around them was settling down and the show was about to begin. The lights dimmed and the show began.

By the time the show ended Elsie was in awe. People were really talented. Just a simple fabric could be turned into so much more that it would leave people gaping. She had taken some photos of some of the designs that she knew she could also tweak here and there, changing the clothing to something different as she felt some of the designs would have looked grander if made in that manner, their loss and her gain. Though she didn't like sewing clothes especially for adults since she felt they had too many specifics, she didn't mind sewing for herself.

The rich pink satin material she was wearing, had called out to her and she couldn't resist dressing up like the rest for the show. It had taken her four hours to complete the attire and she loved the effect including Randy's reaction when he first saw her.

Her mom had mentioned that she could attend this year's fashion gala with her dad Ethan Ross and she couldn't wait. The last time she wanted to, it was postponed due to the lockdown? Now since they were in full swing, it was a must that she went there.

Nita had mentioned the glamour and splendor to be experienced while her eyes had rolled. It's not like she had intended to be a designer before after all.

When she tried out with the lingerie collection it was for fun and Ethan used some of what she made for a fashion show. They loved it and before she knew it, she had changed what she wanted to do. While

Nita was fashion crazy and was already representing some brands as a model, why wouldn't she by the way, after inheriting a tall figure from her father and his side of the family. Nita and Wendy were the tall ones in the family, taking after their father while Elsie was short like her mom.

Elsie had imagined being an English teacher as she would be calmer and not at all wild like her former self. Rita had been shocked by her choice and her fear of doing something that required her to be out there. When she finally told her, her secret, she like everyone else who knew told her to forget. She then insisted she take up a course in fashion after she caught her more than once sketching designs. What she took as her past time hobby became her career choice.

Elsie breathed in the cool fresh air and walked clutching on Randy's arm while they came out of the hall after the show.

Everyone was excited and it could be detected from their faces and voices. A voice was heard calling her name ahead of them. The lights on the campus were brightly lit and she was able to identify Sean leaning against his black Jaguar f-pace with his hands in the pocket. Sean was like her uncle and friends, who had no problem at all in showing that they were loaded.

While she on the other hand had become self-conscious after she was sent to the public school. She didn't want to stand out, apart from her hair color of course. Right now he fitted in easily with all the fancy cars around them and the finery dressing. He was dressed in a slim fit wide pane navy blue suit. As usual he managed to make others in suits look sloppy. He sure could wear a suit as it would snuggly fit his body like a second skin. This time he had added white sneakers. That's as casual as he could be, she thought as she rushed into his arms, glad to see that he had come after all, even though late.

Randy had draped his jacket over her shoulders at seeing that she was shivering a bit when they came out of the hall. He grimaced wondering why he could feel disconcerted at seeing her in her boyfriend's arms. He nodded at Sean.

"Sorry love couldn't be there for the fashion show, I can still take you out for a treat right?" he asked her and she giggled.

"Sure, provided we go with Randy since he was a good sport and agreed to all this."

Sean corked his brow inquiringly and Randy looked at Elsie who shook her head when he was about to protest. "Ok."

"Great" Elsie said and got into Sean's car while Randy went to his and tailed them till they got to the club.

Since it was a Friday, the club was already crowded with youths. They settled on one of the tables before Sean and Randy excused themselves for the bar to get their drinks.

"Hi Elsie" Marcia walked over to her table and greeted her before she sat next to her without being offered a seat. Their families were well acquainted and Marcia happened to be Sean's friend and former classmate. Marcia was tall and beautiful, with long legs and at the moment was dressed in white shorts, light pink chiffon top and red jacket. Elsie rather envied her height; she could do with that tall frame.

"Hey Mash, how is it" she asked.

"Great love, coming from the fashion show and mighty thirsty" she answered back before making herself more comfortable on the chair. She squealed in delight when the drinks were placed on the table and grabbed one before she gulped in down. Elsie shrugged her shoulders while Sean frowned.

"Great Mash, now I will have to wait again in the long queue."

Marcia rolled her eyes before she retorted back, "that's what gentlemen do, they keep on pouring drinks for the ladies."

Sean walked off and Elsie was forced to introduce Marcia to Randy since she appeared to have a glimmer of interest.

"This is Randy" Elsie introduced. She watched them smile at each other before they shook each other's hands.

"Be a darling Randy and add a few drinks, am in the mood to paaaarty" Marcia said with a wink and gulped down the cider without a pause for effect before she reached out to a glass of margarita that had been brought for Elsie.

"The show left me parched," she explained after she had finished with the drink. Elsie rolled her eyes, Marcia could drink like a fish and they both knew it.

"I did see some of the designs made by your young sister Mel, they were creative" Elsie said making conversation. Marcia leaned onto the table and scratched her chin before pointing to the men at the bar.

"Enough about my young sis designs; let's talk about you and those two hunks over there."

"Mashy baby you do not change," Elsie giggled before she looked to where Marcia had pointed. Slowly taking a sip from her drink she decided to leave it at that. As it was she was confused.

She glanced again at both men standing at the bar and gulped; she was definitely in more trouble than she thought.

Both men at the moment appealed to her and were a deep contract to each other, that's what she had thought before. Now they looked like twins with their strong physiques out there.

Sean had removed his jacket in the car and rolled up his sleeve while Randy's jacket was still draped over her shoulders.

She took a sip from her drink. "You like what you are seeing right" Marcia commented after taking note of Elsie ogling both of them.

"It doesn't hurt to look and even sample the goods if you feel like it."

"Marcia!" Elsie gasped in shock. "What Elsie, don't pretend to be an innocent. You do know you can enjoy perfectly with both of them and with me, a four some" she winked and had Elsie choking on a drink and fanning her face since it had suddenly become hot.

She loved the club and it was where she preferred to be on a Friday. Right now it was swarming with youths and was lively. She coughed and took a sip of her drink. This was one of the things she loathed pertaining to her past. The crowd she had once moved in. She frowned after the shock had faded and replied, "I am not that type of girl."

Marcia snorted. "Don't forget I have known you since we were kids. Ok since you are not that type, is Randy single?"

The way Marcia was glancing at him, like a tasty morsel almost made Elsie throw up in her mouth. The hussy was just too forward, she thought. First she had been speaking about a four some and now she wanted to be with Randy, alone.

"He has a girlfriend" she lied through her teeth as Nanas voice drifted through that Randy needed a woman in his life. Marcia would definitely not do, she was too out there. Though the young lady was pretty and had a beautiful body like a model, she didn't know the difference between right and wrong especially in relationships. She would date four guys at the same time and think it was normal behavior. Randy didn't deserve to have such a partner.

"Even if he has one, I rather love the challenge, I think I have a shot" Marcia suggested with a wink, undeterred by Elsie's statement. Elsie almost clawed her eyes out in her mind. She longed more than ever to be out there other than listening to Marcia.

The men got back to the table and settled down as they had their drinks and talked amidst the loud music.

"I want to dance" Marcia announced and stood up before she asked Randy who accepted with a smirk on his face that made Elsie's tummy tie itself into knots.

The hussy giggled as they left for the dance floor and kept on rubbing her attractive body on Randy.

'I can't handle this anymore,' Elsie thought as the giant green monster called envy clawed on her chest.

She cleared her throat after chucking down the margarita before she motioned for Sean to dance with her.

"Darling, I don't dance remember" he said while she rolled her eyes. "No one will notice that you have two left feet, it's crowded."

Sean heaved a sigh and gave in not wanting to argue over that. Elsie could be a pushover; he had feared she would still be angry with him after he told her he was busy.

She had yelled and cut him off after that without waiting for him to explain. She was rather tired of not being a priority in his life and had threatened to hook up with someone else if he wasn't interested. Women could be so dramatic and Elsie was at the top of the pyramid in that regard. The next time he tried calling her, her phone was off.

His cousin brother had been laughing at his expense as he appeared to be the first Compton to care on what women thought about him. He on the other hand believed in buying trinkets for them to make them forget his ways. Bernhard on the other hand felt that it was good to be a one woman person.

Sean had waved off both his cousin's and left work early, expecting Elsie would be back at her parents place, in bed, weeping over their argument as she tended to do, except this time she wasn't deterred at all since when he went to her house, her mother informed him that she had gone to the show with Randy.

He didn't like it one bit. All of a sudden Randy had become this fall back guy who appeared every time he wasn't there for her. Who could fault the dude, Elsie was attractive after all. He hoped that what he was thinking was way off the mark and Randy was just a friend to her.

Tilting her face up when they got to the dance floor and her arms were wrapped around his neck, he tenderly, slowly and thoroughly kissed her, marking his territory. She was his woman.

Randy grimaced at the lovers display and wondered why. Up until today he had always considered Elsie to be like his young sister. Was it the fact that she had toned down and taken him by surprise that had his heart constricting at the sight of her making out with her boyfriend.

Come on Randy, get a grip of yourself, he mentally shook his head and turned to Marcia who was closer to him than appropriate.

She had whispered in his ear a while ago the size of her bra and innocently asked if he wanted to see. Oh, brother, women surprised him. What had the world come to?

She turned and moved her butt seductively dancing closely on his groin. That had him coughing and letting her go. Already he had been sweating at the way she was shimmying and moving around him. He wasn't a eunuch after all to be subjected to all this. Marcia was a beautiful lady.

Even though he might not feel anything for her in terms of love, that didn't mean his body wouldn't respond to her movements and suggestions. Around him, none of the dances seemed appropriate at all and he suddenly felt ancient. This wasn't his kind of scene. He didn't party and attend fancy dress shows. That just wasn't in his nature. Nan had been wrong, he definitely wasn't enjoying this.

"Excuse me, need the gents" he whispered to Marcia before leaving her right there on the dance floor.

Sean was slowly dancing with Elsie when he heard someone clearing her throat next to them only to turn and see his friend standing with arms over her breasts and looking disapprovingly at them. Not again, he thought and instantly knew that his night was going to be just like any other night whenever he would bump into Marcia, a disrupted one. Elsie usually termed Marcia as Sean's stalker. He always thought their meetings are just a coincidence but right now at the moment when she was glaring at them, he really believed Elsie.

"Am at a loose end here guys" she spoke while Elsie giggled. To his chagrin, Marcia caught his arm and sulked, "Sean dance with me, you don't mind right Elsie." She looked imploringly at the younger woman who shrugged in return before asking, "Where is Randy."

"The gents."

Elsie stepped away while Sean frowned at the intrusion and her. She was helpless and they both knew it since Marcia had monopolized them already and was clutching Sean's arm. Marcia could at times act like a spoilt brat.

He watched his girlfriend leave and settle down on their table before turning to Marcia. "You do know you are a drunk party pooper right."

"Forget it Compton and just dance with me," she laughed gently and wrapped her arms around his neck. He was too much of a gentleman, so he sighed and did what she had asked.

Elsie sat for a while, watching what was happening on the dance floor at the same time keeping a close watch on Sean and Marcia. The hussy was just being a pain as usual.

"Hey" Randy addressed her before settling down next to her. "Where is your Mr. Top-notch lawyer?" he asked with a slight curl on his mouth.

Elsie pointedly looked at the dance floor and Randy had the audacity to whistle.

"She is dancing mighty close."

Marcia was clinging to Sean like his second skin and she frowned at the display as she wondered if Sean loved that, since he appeared to not be in the mood of disintangling himself from her clutches. They slowly swayed in harmony to the beat of the slow music now playing and for a person who had stated he had two left feet, it didn't seem like it. Elsie abruptly stood up and walked out while Randy called out to her and grabbed the jacket on the back of the chair. She wasn't listening but was intent in getting out of there as fast as she could.

He managed to catch her at the entrance before he led her to the opposite direction from the parking lot. "I didn't mean to offend you with my comment" he said. She shrugged her shoulders dismissively.

"Elsie Cooper, I am surprised though."

"Why?" Elsie asked and stopped walking. "I see you are not the kind of girl who would bash another for dancing shamelessly with her man."

"Ooh please, I trust Sean as for Marcia she can dance like that but Sean will never leave me for the likes of her."

"For someone unconcerned your voice mightily shrieks my princess" he chuckled and received a punch on his arm.

"Ouuch" he dragged out, "what was that for?"

"For being so mean" she retorted. She rubbed her arms, feeling the cool air whip against her dress.

Randy draped his jacket on her shoulders and she inhaled the spicy masculine scent of the lapel while they started walking again. "Why did you leave Mashy girl on the dance floor. You are the cause of her bulldozing us."

Randy laughed before he replied, "Mashy girl is just out there, I suddenly realized I don't fit in such a setting."

"Poor Randy," she whispered in understanding. That's what appealed to her even more; Randy was set in his ways and also was more grounded. Whoever he would marry one day would have got a real gem of a man if ever they were anything like that.

"Since Marcia is out, I am sure we can find someone much better." She could hear Randy inhale noisily before he breathed out and turned to face her. "If Marcia is a choice, I had rather not hear the rest." She giggled, quiet enjoying his outraged face. "Why not?" she asked. He rolled his eyes, "Your Mashy girl offered me much more than I have ever been offered after a drink."

"Welcome to the real world," Elsie said and punched him on the shoulder.

"By the way, I thought you once mentioned to me and Rita that you liked a woman with experience."

"I change my mind."

He placed his finger under her chin and tilted her head while her breath hitched at the way he was looking at her.

"An inexperienced one will do much better."

He smiled and that cute dimple appeared.

A voice was heard calling her and Randy dropped his hand from her face before he turned to where the voice was coming from. It was Sean leading Marcia with her arm around him as she looked like one who would topple down any moment. He seemed to realize that and picked her up while they walked towards him.

"I hope you don't mind Randy, please drop Elsie at her place while I take Marcia home" he advised with a scowl. "I will see you tomorrow," he pointedly looked her way before walking to his car. Elsie was about to protest but seeing he had turned away from her, she dropped her hand and tightly clenched it into a fist by her side. He seemed angry and she hoped he hadn't seen that she had been about to kiss Randy. As it was, she was embarrassed over her actions. She had no right to be involved with two men.

"Shall we," Randy asked and she nodded. The drive back home was a quiet one. When they arrived she smiled at Randy after she got out of the car and handed him the jacket.

"Thanks Randy, there is no need for you to accompany me to the door."

"Good night then" Randy smiled reassuringly at her before he drove off. When she got into the house, her mother was still up waiting for her.

"How did it go" she asked. Elsie strode into the living room and settled down on the couch before removing her high heeled shoes.

"The fashion show was a blast as to be expected. Sean showed up and we went to the club. Marcia also showed up." She rolled her eyes at that while her mother chuckled.

"Marcia is sooo grrrh" she groaned while her mother laughed.

"I thought you said Sean wasn't interested in her."

"I know, I know, but you know Mashy babe and from elementary school she always wanted all the attention to be on her."

"And you don't" her mother asked with a raised brow.

"Off course I don't." She bristled.

Her mother snorted. "Don't you think you have been spending too much of your time with Randy?"

"Yes, it's because Sean is not always available ma."

She could see concern on her face but she wasn't going to listen to her warning. This was her problem, one way or the other she would end up with the man she thought was good enough for her. If it meant she had to bid her time in figuring that out. So be it, but she wasn't going to allow any of them to date while she figured out her confusion.

"You do know you can't replace someone's lack of attention by using another right?"

"Ma...I am not using Randy, he is... just my friend."

Her mother heaved a sigh before she got up from the recliner, "I hope so darling."

She moved to where Elsie sat and kissed her on the forehead.

"Good night love, don't forget to switch off the lights" she advised before walking away, back to bed.

It was after she was done with her toiletry and getting into bed when her phone rang. "Hey, just checking up whether you made it safe home." Sean asked.

"Yes, I arrived in one stitch." She giggled and heard him huff. "Elsie is something going on between you and Randy." Sean didn't beat around the bush and his tone definitely sounded irritated.

"Nothing is going on."

"Well it didn't look like nothing. I know love you can be a flirt but this is different."

"Relax Sean, nothing is going on."

"If you say so." He sounded tired and resigned.

"Sean remember what I said, you can walk away any time you want."

Ever since she told him about her past, that seemed to have shifted the relationship somehow. It was no longer the same and she had wished she had taken that about herself to the grave.

"I love you Elsie," he said. "I know I might have a funny way of showing it but I do."

"Ok," she said and hung up. She knew she was not being fair to Sean but knew he was the only one who could accept her whole heartedly. She feared if she truly opened up to Randy he would no longer look at her the way he had done tonight. Life was just so complicated, she thought before she reached out to her side lamp and switched it off.

Sean unbuttoned his shirt and grimaced. He hoped Elsie was right in saying that there was nothing between her and Randy. As it was, Elsie appeared to be the best choice he had made according to his father. He knew the only reason his father was impressed is because he hoped to gain more connections from the Cooper, Ross and Henderson relations he was likely to have once Sean and Elsie got married.

Its time he went out for a reprieve, out of town to unwind. He couldn't do that at home since his father happened to be a slave driver and a workaholic. He sure would enjoy being around Clark and Will his childhood friends. With that in mind, he punched in a reminder on his phone. Next week he would make the journey and he hoped he would also have clarity over his relationship with Elsie.

Chapter Four

ELSIE WOKE up early the next day to a chaotic atmosphere as usual. Her noisy young sisters and brother.

"Hey Eric" she greeted when she came out of the room and hugged her little brother before swinging him in her arms as he laughed in delight.

Laura cried also, "me too" while Elsie rolled her eyes.

"You are too heavy poppet" she answered and her six year old young sis pouted and her eyes became watery. She was tinny for her age like all of them actually because of their mother's tiny and short stature so Elsie sighed out of resignation and swung her into her arms to her delight before she did the same with Lorraine.

"Morning Thelma" she straightened and greeted the maid who nodded to her while the children escaped to the other room.

"Any plans for the day?" her mother asked as she got into the kitchen.

"I was thinking of visiting Randy's granny today."

Her mother frowned at that. So Elsie was going to be obstinate and not take her advice.

"Relax ma, am just visiting an old woman only, nothing more to it."

"If you say so." Her mother answered but Elsie could tell from her expression that she didn't like that one bit.

It's not like she would see Randy. He was a busy person. Her tummy fluttered at the thought of the almost kiss. Randy's interest would fizzle out if he came to know the kind of girl she was.

Jealousy had clawed on her heart when he smiled at Marcia before they left for the dance floor. Yet as usual Randy was the perfect gentleman with Marcia including stepping away when she plastered her body around him.

Her attention had been focused on them while on the dance floor and not at all on Sean, though she did enjoy the kiss.

Sean was skilled when he kissed and that usually made her bones melt. It was a surprise that she hadn't given him much more than a kiss in the four years they had been together.

She thought back on when he asked her to be his girlfriend. He was a freshman at law school and definitely one of the coolest guys according to her. He was sophisticated and appealed to her in more ways than one. Especially when she rubbed the girls faces in that fact at school. Girls who appeared to strive on thinking themselves better than anyone else. Thanks to her mom and strict ways, she couldn't show the snotty girls that she was way above them by all means.

She had never suffered from lack of confidence before when it came to dealing with other girls at the private school she was once at, but those middle class girls truly knew on how to blow their trumpets, even with fewer things than she had.

Thanks to Sean when he dropped by at the school gate he managed to silence them all, in his orange sports car another of his collection and a tight bod in black trousers, white shirt slightly open on the chest and a red blazer.

Finally they had realized who they were dealing with and she was so ready to chuck out the ordinary uniform and dress in all her finery.

Sean was a virgin and wanted to remain that till they got married. He opened up about his family and how he didn't want to follow the trend. He was trying to be unique. Elsie had felt disquieted after he mentioned that. He thought she was an innocent. It took her two years to finally open up and she had thought he would leave after he found out about the kind of girl she was except Sean stuck around her with her craziness, her tumultuous emotions and her flirting ways. She loved to do that a lot but it never got out of hand. She just loved the attention bestowed on her by men.

"Can we come with you Elsie" Lorraine asked having overheard that bit in the conversation. Elsie knew her mother already doubted her intentions hence she quickly nodded while her sister screamed and went to get ready informing Laura who was playing with Eric.

Eric wailed when he saw his playmates leave the house and his mother held him back by whispering that they would buy him ice cream on their way back.

Such was Elsie's surprise when she got to Randy's place and it was abuzz with activity.

"What is going on?" she asked Nana once she got into the house with the twins.

"A family brunch of some sort. We used to have these while Randy's parents were still alive" she answered. Lilly and Raff got into the kitchen and hugged her before they left with the twins to meet their other relations.

"Surprise!!" Rita yelled by the door and Elsie stood up, indeed surprised at seeing her there. "I can't believe this Rita, when did you arrive from uni. Thought you had forgotten about us simple folks after getting into the prestigious med school."

"You wish" she giggled and gave her a hug. "I did send a voicemail yesterday. Why are you here then if you didn't get it?" Her brow furrowed while Elsie swiftly waved off the question and asked on whether she now had a boyfriend. Nan chuckled at Rita's expression. "Rita just like Randy isn't searching until she finishes her studies."

"Which of course nana thinks is absurd" Rita added before moving to settle next to the old lady. Elsie joined her and asked, "Nan, how do you know that you are ready to commit to a person and also that the one you have chosen is 'the one' that you have been searching for" she used her fingers to that effect, quoting on 'the one' part.

"How did you know that you were going to commit for four years to Sean?" Rita interrupted as usual while Elsie resisted the urge to roll her eyes and expectantly waited for the old woman to answer. They were interrupted by Randy's cousins who burst into the kitchen before Nan answered and dragged outside to join the rest of the family. In all that time Elsie hadn't caught a glimpse of Randy. They were a lot of things taking place. Rita's family was also there and Dustin was playing the music while others danced.

Elsie was introduced to the cousin sisters and brothers, aunts and uncles and had a blast. It hadn't been what she had expected when she left home but she was glad that the twins also had fun and were dancing with the other children their age.

"So how is big daddy Sean?" Rita asked her while they were settled on the steps leading to the backyard and watching the family on the grounds. The children were dancing while the adults were still having their meal. Nan had also joined them and was chatting with two old women. Elsie and Rita were done with their meal. Rita handed Elsie a can of cola before reaching out for another one and opening it.

"He is fine, the last time I checked."

"And when was that" her friend asked.

"Yesterday."

"Hmmm for a person who was once madly in love, you appear not to chat about Sean as much as you used to. What's going on?" With the way she was looking at her, Elsie giggled and answered, "Nothing is going on."

"Ok, if you say so. You will tell me if there is something wrong right. Like an old flame coming into the picture?" Rita joked and they both burst into fits of laughter. "Do share the joke" Randy spoke from behind them and Elsie felt her tummy flutter in response to his voice. She shifted so he could pass them and stand in front of them. He was dressed in an indigo V-neck shirt that tautly stretched over his body as usual and black ripped jeans. Whoever mentioned to him that his body was attractive had ruined Elsie's chances of being sane around him.

"None of your biz" Rita retorted good humoredly.

"Rita don't forget you are in my territory and I have every right to know." She scoffed and rolled her eyes while Elsie did nothing to help her out. "I think Dustin the dj is calling me," Rita finally said, standing up and moving away before she turned and hollered, "It's up to you Elsie to handle him."

Randy sighed at the dramatic way Rita was before he settled down next to Elsie and nudged her by the shoulders.

"What!!"

"What were you talking about?"

Elsie scoffed and retorted. "Definitely not about you."

"You are beautiful you know that?" Randy asked her with a grin and made her blush instead as she lowered her eyes.

He was glad to see her there. After last night his opinion of her from being like his young sis suddenly took a 360 degree turn. He noticed also what he had been blind to before, her attraction to him. Not that he had been blind, but he always brushed it aside thinking it was just a phase. Only God knew what went on around Elsie's mind. She appeared to enjoy though coming to his neighborhood for a visit.

"Sooo how is Marcia?"

Elsie frowned before she shrugged her shoulders and answered, "I don't know, why do you ask?"

"I figured I would save you the time and effort for looking for a woman for me like Nan suggested and you give me her number."

She huffed, "If I remember correctly yesterday you didn't want anything to do with the lady."

"I changed my mind, I slept on her suggestion and I woke up thinking she is what I want."

He smothered a laugh when Elsie opened her mouth and shut it without uttering a word. She was jealous, he knew it. One thing still bothered him though, if her relationship with Sean was that serious, why were they not married. He understood the whole concept of waiting till she was done with varsity yet at the same time felt if he were Sean he wouldn't wait for that long.

Like his Nan, he knew the temptations involved with couples dating for a longer time. He had tried it and before long, his girlfriend wanted to get him into bed. He decided to focus on one thing at a time and forget about relationships. One thing he wanted was to be a role model to his siblings by marrying a good girl, believer like him and who chose to wait for sex and did it in a marriage setting than what their generation termed as 'trying out.'

Already some of his friends whined over women cramping their style. They decided to sleep around without much thought of the consequence and were now married to women they did not even like, while he on the other hand enjoyed being single. He could do what he liked and wasn't answerable to anyone, especially with his money. Soon he would be opening up his new garage as he had managed to save a bit.

"You were right Marcia is definitely not your type, nope." she shook her head in denial.

"Why not. She is attractive, fun to be with and a hell of a great dancer."

"Marcia is too forward Randy" Elsie scoffed. Now it was her repeating the same words that he had said the previous night. What was up with Randy she wondered?

"I don't think so" he paused while she opened her mouth to refute and closed it without commenting. "She is experienced in other areas also, and she was more than willing to offer..." he leaned in and whispered in her ear. Elsie gasped in shock.

"I think I should get a stronger drink," Elsie said abruptly standing up and walking away. Randy was just full of it, she thought. If he wanted that kind, she could definitely be that for him. It's not like she had forgotten the mechanics of lovemaking in the seven years she had been chaste. What was she even thinking; she had made a promise to God to confine those intimacies to marriage and nothing else.

She was reaching out for a can of beer in the refrigerator when Nan came into the kitchen also. "What are you looking for here, thought you were out enjoying with the rest."

"I just needed this." She pulled out the two cans and showed them to Nan before settling down on the kitchen chair. She much preferred the old woman's company to Randy's naughty one, especially after the suggestion he had made.

"They is nothing like 'the one', you can make it with anyone you wish to in a relationship." Nan said and Elsie remembered the question she had asked before they had been interrupted. "Nan that can't be right, I mean we hear success stories of happily ever after and you are saying they isn't that perfect one. We can make it work with whoever we want to be with."

The music could be clearly heard and the voices drifting in, but for the mean time she felt they had the privacy to talk before they were interrupted. A sharp nod came from the old woman before she answered, "How did you know that Rita could be your friend?"

"Well Rita is kind and we get along quite well. We have some things in common that we bond on and also we are two different people hence complement each other at the same time."

"A love relationship is the same like any other relationship. Imagine if both of you took from your relationship while you expected the other party to be a doormat. Instead of being patient with each other about ones weaknesses but having a critical nature all the time, what would happen?"

"Well Nan my friendship with Rita is different from my love relationship with Sean."

"How is it different? You put the same things that you feed the other relationship. They are all relationships with people. So those who you think have it all made up and found 'the one' did the same in their relationship, they cultivated those basics that you require in any relationship including with friends or family. Things like love, loyalty, honesty, patience, faithfulness and respect."

"So I am really not going to find the one then?" she waved her hands and Nan chuckled.

"You will find that man who appeals to you more than the rest. The question is.... are you willing to keep that up in the long-haul. Be fascinated in the same manner that you were when you first met or just like everything else it will die down since you would have become familiar and stopped being impressed. What do you kids of nowadays call it, falling out of love?"

Elsie giggled at that, the old woman was just being narrow minded in her thinking yet deep down what she was speaking about resonated within her.

"I love you but I am not 'in' love with you. There is nothing like that."

Elsie decided to open one of the cans. She needed that drink after all. "What if you happened to be in love with two men? What then since you are saying there is nothing like that?"

"You will need to get your head screwed on straight" Nan jested and Elsie giggled.

"You need to ask yourself on why do you feel that way and take a stand back. At times it means if you were in a relationship with both, you leave both guys because in the first place you never had time to get to know them. You just chose the good parts about them and forgot the rest. It's either you love a person fully but you can't give them half of you."

Elsie thought back to one of the conversation she once had with Rita as she had echoed the same sentiments. "Most of the time it's about you and the fact that you are not satisfied with what you have and who you are that causes that. You will be interested in this guy because they have the money but he can't satisfy you in another way, that guy because he has time for you but he can't buy you the trinkets you love. You need to find contentment in yourself and not search it out from someone else; no human is perfect to fill out whatever you might want. If it's that what you want only one man can fill up that need, our Lord Jesus Christ."

Rita burst into the kitchen yelling, "Your favorite song is playing."

"Go on" Nan waved her hands chuckling at the same time. Elsie hugged her before she left and whispered, "thank you."

She rolled her eyes at Rita who was taping the floor with her shoe at the door impatiently waiting for her. "Let's go" she grabbed her hand and they rushed to the backyard and were in time to see everyone lined up and dancing to the song.

Chapter Five

ELSIE LOOKED around the restaurant and heaved a sigh before taking a peek at her wrist watch. She doubted Randy would show up after she called him at the last minute. She missed Nita and wished she was there with her as Nita tended to take her up on her last minute plans. Rita had called to apologize, she had an exam on Monday so wouldn't be able to travel to and from school for the weekend.

Sean as usual was busy with work. It was two weeks after the brunch at Randy's place and the sage advice she had received from Nan. She had taken that advice to heart and decided to give a last chance to her relationship except Sean was always busy. Last week he took the trip to go and visit his friends and came back looking great and well rested.

She knew he drove himself hard to impress his dad, but rather felt that he wasn't living his life because of it. She rather thought his dad will always be unimpressed no matter how hard Sean tried. She had visited her father and his wife over the weekend with the twins and they loved the more amicable Luc. He took them out for some burgers so he could just get a taste of meat, since his diet conscious wife had put him on a veggy diet. Everyone was laughing at the steak he ordered and especially when he bribed the twins not to tell.

She glanced at the door again for the umpteenth time before her gaze riveted back to the surrounding tables. Happy people with their families and friends, good conversation, laughter and soft live music drifting from the back ground as one of the local singers did what they knew best. This would be a first time for Randy to stand her up. After their talk over what he wanted, she thought he might have wiggled out Marcia's number from Sean and had called her.

His nana had mentioned that he had taken out an unknown lady for a couple of movies during the week and jealousy had clawed at her heart nearly shredding it into mincemeat. Nan had the nerve to laugh over her strident voice on the phone when she wanted the full details. Nan was going to be the death of her. The old woman had easily pointed out, "You are working out on your relationship with Sean remember."

She was still surprised over how free she was with Nana and would tell her everything, including her fears, hopes and dreams. Nan was just one of those people who never judged. The old woman knew a lot on what the youths were up to and tended to point out with a laugh that she was once a youngster also.

Elsie was relieved when she spotted Randy and flagged him to where she sat. She continued observing him as his tall frame drew closer. Rita had felt it was a bad idea for her to meet up with him; she was worried that she would make a mess of their friendship with her confused love, but her advice had fallen on deaf ears. If Sean couldn't be there, then Randy was the best alternative. Dressed in coffee jeans, white t-shirt, checkered black and white shirt with his unshaven beard, he was quite a looker. It seemed he had grown back his beard after the fashion show.

"Hey Randy, thanks for coming at such a short notice."

Randy smiled before he settled down and remarked, "I wouldn't miss out on a free meal."

He winked at her and she crossed her legs. She had already ordered the pizza and it didn't take long after he had settled down for the waiter to bring it to their table including the sodas and fried chicken. The workers knew her since she was at her uncle's jazz club cum restaurant, Greg's.

"Are you expecting more people" Randy asked with a corked brow after taking in the food that the waiter had brought.

"Nope it's just the two of us."

"Ah huh, are you on a feeding scheme here or are you expecting?"

She blushed at the thought before she answered, "Oh you, stop goofing around and eat. I happen to like letting go and eating my fill on a Friday. As for being pregnant, you wish. I and Sean don't share that kind of relationship."

She smothered a laugh at his surprised face and gaped mouth. Geez, did men think about sex all the time that it sounded alien if they heard that one wasn't doing it. Randy cleared his throat before he asked, "Where is our Mr. Top-notch lawyer by the way."

"Busy as usual."

"Come on you have to be kidding, he can't be busy all the time that he can't even make time for his girl."

"That's Sean for you" she shrugged her shoulders dismissively before taking a bite of the chicken thigh. How she loved the aromatic spicy taste. She moaned and giggled at the fact that Randy had rolled his eyes. She liked the beard but its shadow not the full one which she thought definitely needed a trim and fast, was he trying to win some kind of beard contest or what, her mind thought while the other part of her mind took in everything else around her. So much for trying to be content, it was official, she and Sean were over. She had dragged that long enough.

Randy took a sip of his drink before asking about her day. In no time they were talking about everything happening in their lives.

Randy treated her in the same way he had before and she wondered if how he had acted at the club, the surprise over her hair had been just that and that euphoria had faded. She was disappointed though at the fact that he was back to his usual self. She would have wanted a Randy who could be naughty. Discontent, discontent, she thought and sighed. At least on a better note by Randy being his normal self it meant she was safe and he didn't think of her as being forward and slutty at the fact that she would cheat on Sean in a heartbeat. The same Sean she had been thinking it was over. Her safety net.

"Earth to Elsie" Randy waved his hand in front of her face. She giggled before she apologized, "sorry my mind had wandered off."

"I guess I am boring company then" Randy said to her with a smirk. She took a sip of her soda instead, relieved that he hadn't read into what she might be thinking.

"No you will never be that and you know it," she answered and was in time to hear people clap after the singer completed their song.

On Friday's the club usually had a Karaoke night and as expected after the local upcoming artist finished singing the floor was left for the guests. It was either singing or poetry. Uncle Greg's Jazz club strived in that while Uncle Dominic's family had a small cozy theatre out of town. She had usually gone there just to watch plays written out by upcoming script and play writers.

She had caught her mom and dad speaking about some charity event that they wanted to do over the holidays as Wendy had written out a modern-day version of Cinderella and they thought it would make youths appreciate that side of art. She couldn't wait.

A sudden thought came into mind when the person speaking on the microphone asked on who wanted to sing first. She raised her hand, giggling at Randy's outraged face. "Ok, we have our first singer for the night. Folks let us give a round of applause for Elsie and her friend."

She stood up and grabbed Randy's hand.

He would have wished to protest but with the people watching, silently walked to the stage and stood awkwardly near a microphone while Elsie spoke with the deejay. She finally came next to him and whispered, "I love old school, hope you don't mind that I selected the prayer by Celine Dion." She muffled a laugh when he rolled his eyes before he nodded. She looked back, nodded to the deejay and the sound drifted through, loud and clear. The words flashed on the side on the screen near where they stood, but she didn't need to read at all, since she knew it by heart.

She giggled as Randy looked like he would escape from there any moment before she started singing.

She knew her voice was passable and she could hold a note. When it was Randy's turn her eyes opened widely in surprise at the first note. Not fair, he had been pretending when the guy could send shivers down her spine with his voice. His loud melodious voice boomed and he tilted his head staring at her and winked before nodding his head signaling they had to sing together on the chorus. She cleared her throat and joined him, marveling at the way their voices blended perfectly together.

Silence issued when they were done before a huge round of applause followed and a few whistles. Randy winked at her and she giggled before curtseying and they walked away back to their table which had now been cleared of their dishes. She took her seat and looked at Randy still surprised at what had just happened.

"Why are you looking at me as if I committed a crime?"

"You know you did," she continued staring at him accusingly, "You forgot to mention that you could sing. Look I even have goose bumps because of that." She motioned to her arns while Randy shrugged his shoulders dismissively. "Oh that it's nothing; I used to be in the school choir in high school."

How could he be so casual about it? She thought and decided to tease him so she got the reaction she wanted, a surprised one like her.

"I think I should add that on the qualities section of your profile."

Randy rolled his eyes. She was daring him. He didn't want to shock her when he made his interests known. He rather loved the fact she had disclosed about her relationship with Sean, that it wasn't that deep.

Finally he answered, "What you and nana need are lives of your on, active ones so you stop trying to meddle into mine."

Elsie huffed, "Well sorry Randy, I promised nana that by the end of the month you will be dating and I will make sure I deliver. Heard from Nan also that you were out on a few dates. So I don't think my additions will hurt that much or cramp your style."

Randy scoffed while she giggled. "Good luck then in your new venture, I will not discourage you."

"At least you know when to concede," she muttered playfully before speaking loud enough for him to hear, "For starters we should change your appearance."

"What's wrong with my appearance?" Randy frowned and scratched his beard before crossing his arms over his chest. He looked intimidating especially if he happened to glare at her. She nervously laughed and cleared her throat, "well I can't say if you look at me in that manner, it's rather intimidating."

At that he chuckled.

"Can you hear that," she said and he leaned in with a raised brow. "Randy, Randy, Randy, we need a trim," she whispered and winked. Randy laughed a deep throated laugh. He knew he will never have a dull day in his life with Elsie in it. He could just imagine her using the same tactic on the children so they could go and bath.

"I guess I am not that intimidating, if my beard still complains. I am just little old me."

She scoffed, "little, Randy can you even see yourself." She motioned with her hand from his head where he sat and glared at him before continuing, "You are strong, muscular, tall..."

As she spoke Randy shifted and moved his chair closer before he placed his right elbow on his thigh and cradled his cheek so he could look at her intently while she rambled. She could feel the heat rise up to her face as she blushed at his attention. That was a forbidden route to take, her to think of Randy and his male physique and voice it out to him.

"What else princess" he softly spoke with a light glimmer in his eyes as his voice reverberated and she felt its impact over her body. She drew her collar with one of her fingers away from her throat.

"Stop it" she blurted out, only to raise her eyes and see him sipping on his drink with a raised brow. Did she just imagine all that? She sat back and fanned her face. The restaurant was rather getting hot, she thought. She couldn't have imagined that, since she could see that they now sat closely together and Randy appeared to be concentrating ahead to two girls who were singing on stage.

She swallowed, although she had wished to catch a glimpse of that side of him. She now was having second thoughts. Even Sean didn't make her feel that way when he was just talking and without touching her. He fanned her feelings by kissing her.

He turned to look at her and asked, "Anything the matter princess, thought we were still talking about my good qualities."

Chuckling, she pretended to be listening to another person who had now gone on stage before turning to him and remarking, "I wouldn't want you to be like a proud rooster after that, enough about your qualities."

"Fine, enough about you trying to set me up with a woman" he retorted back.

"Why not, you need a good woman like your nana says."

"My nana says a lot of things." Randy held the back of her chair and easily shifted it so she now faced him instead. She could feel her heart rate rise as he drew her seat closer.

"Don't do that or else?" The threat was in his voice that had become a whisper while her senses reeled in shock and her skin literally prickled at the closeness.

"Or else what?" she bluffed. This time her eyes widened as he leaned in to her ear and she felt the beard slightly brush against her sensitive cheek before he whispered "or else I will make you fall deeply in love with me, that you will stop trying to find that lady." He sat back, smiled before he turned her chair back to its position. A jumble of butterflies could be felt fluttering in her tummy. Randy had returned to cheering the singer who was done and another one went up the stage.

Rita had been wrong, Randy was indeed that guy who had want to make her forget everything like she had thought before. He had the naughty side that he managed to hide from the rest of the people around him. Although her friend would not believe if she told her what had taken place, she definitely would have to find a way to prove it. She hadn't told her about the near kiss, but this dare was going to be proof enough.

Glancing at him through the corner of her eye, Randy didn't seem at all unnerved as she was. Rather it was as if he hadn't said anything out of the ordinary and everything was as it was meant to be. Be in control, get a grip of yourself, she muttered under her breath and pasted on a smile.

She couldn't be defeated now when things suddenly appeared to have taken a twist. The thrill of the cat and mouse game suddenly appealed to her more.

"I will look for that woman," she said and watched him smirk before he retorted, "Get ready, I hope you don't live to regret this day" before he winked at her and she almost clutched at her tummy as the sensation increased.

He motioned for her in question if they could leave and she nodded. Paying up the bill, she almost protested but stopped at his glare. He wasn't the type to let a lady pay. She had draped her denim jacket on the chair; Randy reached for it and helped her wear it. A slight brush of his finger on her shoulders managed to send some shivers down her spine and she caught herself having crossed her legs. Why did she have to have her father's blood coursing through out her body? She could feel her smile was wobbly and she looked up to Randy and he had a glimmer in his eyes. He knew what she was thinking.

"Shall we?" she said before walking ahead of him, out of the place and breathing in the fresh cool air when she finally got outside.

She once watched an old movie Hitch, starring Will Smith and Eva Mendes with her mother. She was having that same feeling that the other woman might have felt, standing at the doorstep and twirling her keys around.

While she stood at the door of her car, she thought about that particular scene and how the guy was meant to kiss the lady then. Randy was looking at her intently, he leaned over and she shut her eyes. She caught a whiff of his musky cologne and could feel his body heat encompassing her.

He cleared his throat and she opened her eyes still in a daze before everything came to a standstill and stopped whirling around her, butterflies and all. "Your ride awaits princess," Randy said with a chuckle and Elsie realized that he had opened her door for her while she had been acting silly and anticipating a kiss.

She was contemplating on how to react at the fact that, he was still the solicitous guy and didn't look at all like a person who had threatened to make her fall in love with him. "Elsie, do you love my company that much to the point you are not in the mood to go home?"

Her eyes widened and she punched him on the chest. "Ha, ha, don't think too much about yourself. Goodnight." She whispered and got into her car. Since he was still watching her, she couldn't sit back and relax, shut her eyes and think about him. She cheerily waved at him and drove off. By the time Elsie got home, her pulse had normalized and she knew her inquisitive mother wouldn't ask any of those out of the blue kind of questions. After getting out of the car, she slowly walked to the door, imagining what could have been.

Chapter Six

THE DOOR to the house was abruptly opened, it was her step dad. "Hey princess, how was your date." She shrugged before getting into the house, "So, so was with Randy since Sean couldn't make it."

"About that....." he followed behind her as she came to a sudden halt in the living room. Sean was settled on the couch, looking handsome as always in his three piece black pinstripe slim fit suit. "Hey love," he greeted her and stood up. She rushed into his arms yet at the same time feeling nervous. Why was he there all of a sudden?

"Sean wants to say something to you," her step dad spoke and joined her mother on the other couch before putting his arms around her. Her mother almost looked like someone who was about to shed a few tears, what was happening?

"Sean, what is going on," her brow furrowed as she watched him kneel and produce the velvet tiny box. Oh my God, she thought, shocked at the unexpected turn of events. This couldn't be happening. Didn't they agree with Sean that she would have to complete varsity first before this happened. What had suddenly brought this on? What about Randy?

"Elsie, as you know we have been dating for four years. I know we have our ten year plan, but since we will do this in future I thought why not now. I asked your parents and they are happy, now the decision is up to you." He coughed and cleared his throat while she nervously laughed when her mother instantly produced a glass of water that he took appreciatively and gulped down. Knowing Sean, this was harder to do since he wasn't one to express his feelings that easily.

"I love you and want to spend the rest of my life with you. So will you do me the honor of becoming my wife?"

She chewed at the inside of her bottom lip suddenly having an image of Randy threatening to make her fall for him. She looked to her parents who were beaming and her handsome boyfriend. The past months had been a blur as she had lost her focus. She swore she would never be like her father, a man who struggled to commit to one woman. Four years was long and they had made it with Sean.

Sean was smiling at her, not at all the unconcerned guy she at times thought him to be. She could see that he loved her and she wasn't going to disappoint him.

"Yes" she finally answered and he placed the ring on her finger before standing up and kissing her.

"And there I thought you would refuse."

She chuckled as he hugged her and her mother hugged her dad. She turned to them and held up her hand; "I am getting married" she squealed and went over to hug them. They hugged Sean also, "Congrats son and welcome to the family," her step dad said. "We will leave you to talk a bit," her mother said before leaving with her dad for their room.

"This was a surprise," she said while Sean smiled. He twined her fingers with his before giving her a kiss on the back of the hand. "We will be happy together love. I should go home and inform my parents."

Nodding her head at that, she accompanied him to the door and kissed him before watching him walk to the car. After she shut the door she rushed upstairs to her room. Sean was the one for her, they had dated for four years and it wasn't worth it to lose all that because all of a sudden she had begun to see Randy in a new light. Her parents loved Sean and they loved Randy also. God what was she doing, she thought and decided to give a call to her friend who would bring clarity to her jumbled up thoughts. She couldn't tell Rita of her feelings to Randy in that they ran deeper than she had anticipated; she might get angry with her for dragging him along yet knowing fully well that she would eventually get married to Sean.

She cleared her throat and at the third ring her friend answered. "Guess what Rita!!' she managed to sound happy, she was after all getting married. "What?" her friend asked with a chuckle.

"You have to guess, duh."

Rita answered, "Jaden Smith asked for your hand in marriage." Elsie giggled. "Close but not that close."

She could hear her friend gasp before she asked, "Sean asked you to marry him?"

"Yes he did." They was a long pause that made her wonder what was going on before Rita's voice finally drifted through, "Congratulations my friend, am happy for you."

"Thanks love. It took me by surprise though, wasn't expecting it. You my dear are going to be my chief bridesmaid, so you have to get ready for bridezilla on the prowl," she said and could hear Rita laughing also. "You bet I am happy for you. Can we chat some other time was still catching up on some work?"

"It's okay love," Elsie said before she said good night and hung up.

After her call with Rita she got ready for bed and was coming out of the bathroom when her door was slightly opened. It was Laura her young sis.

"Hey love, are you not meant to be in bed, sleeping?" she asked and watched her young sister pull the covers on her bed before she got in. She grinned showing her a gap toothed smile before asking "what happened why was mommy crying before getting into her room."

Elsie chuckled; her emotional mom must have been tearing up after she left them downstairs. Elsie got into bed and hugged her young sister before showing her the diamond ring. "Mommy is happy because I got this from Sean. He wants to marry me."

Laura pouted her cute little mouth at hearing that. Elsie thinking she hadn't understood continued to explain, "Remember the weddings we attended so far where you and Lorrain had to bear rings for a couple. That is what Sean and I will be doing in a few months' time."

"I know what to marry is, why Sean?" her little brow had furrowed. Elsie giggled before answering, "why not Sean. We love each other."

"Sean is always scolding me and Lorrain, frowning as if he would spank us. Why not Randy, we like his family more."

Elsie chuckled, if it was the date my family show, she knew who her young sisters would choose.

"You two are naughty that's why. But Sean is a good person."

Laura nodded and snuggled up to her sister before asking "So does it mean you are leaving home?"

Elsie nodded and watched her young sister pull from her embrace before she did a little jig on the bed. "Why are you dancing?"

"I get to have a room of my own."

Elsie was so outraged by the time she got up from the covers her young sister had already escaped to the door and darted her tongue out. "Traitor" she shouted before Laura dashed back to her room that she shared with Lorraine. And there she had been thinking her young sister would miss her. By Laura's reaction she knew her young brother will be excited over cake, Lorrain over not having to share a room with her twin. Maybe the ones who would actually miss her would be Wendy and Nita who were still at boarding and slightly maybe Marilyn. Marilyn had finally adjusted to boarding life and appeared to not care at all about them after making some friends; hence Elsie doubted very much that her marriage would make a difference.

This was Nita's last year at high school before she ventured out into the world. How time seemed to fly. And she was to be married. Her phone rang startling her. It might be Sean; she thought and reached out to it.

"Princess." Her heart fluttered and she found herself clutching at the phone for comfort. She should have checked the name before getting it and now they was no way to hang up. "Just making sure you travelled safe."

"I did Randy and thanks for the great time."

"My pleasure," he answered. Her toes curled at his voice and she burrowed into her blankets. "Guess who I found when I got home," she nervously asked.

"Who, your top notch lawyer boyfriend."

"Ye-e-s" she stuttered. How did Randy seem to know her so well? "He asked me to marry him," she paused but Randy didn't say anything so she continued, "I accepted."

She could have wished for Randy to tell her that she was making the wrong decision and choose him. Instead Randy cheerfully congratulated her. "I am happy for you princess, Sean is good for you."

Elsie found herself losing her patience and becoming irritated. Was this all he could say. Of all things for a man who had said he would make her fall in love with him, he was easily giving her up.

"Ok, let me rest, it was a long day today" she spoke with her voice dripping in sarcasm.

"Good night princess and sweet dreams" he said and hung up. Huh! She looked at her phone for a while. So that was it. Her sad unrequited love story. One moment she had thought he was also in love with her and now she doubted. She threw the phone on the bed frustrated and she had thought her mother was the confused one. Guess the saying was true. Like mother like daughter and right now she wished more than ever to love and settle for one man like she had done at the end.

Chapter Seven

"MORNING MA" Elsie greeted, getting into the kitchen and settled on the bar stool.

"Hey love, how was your night?"

"It was good." She took the hot coffee that her mother slid to her and inhaled the sweet aroma before taking a sip. "I will surely miss this."

Her mother chuckled and moved to the shelf, took two dinner plates. She dished out the hot bacon and scrambled eggs before joining her on the kitchen counter.

"Next you will be doing this for Sean's family."

At that statement her appetite seemed to deflate. What was going on with her? She should be happy that her boyfriend of four years had proposed but here she was thinking of someone else and how he had reacted to the news.

'Congratulations princess, am happy for you.' Is that all he could say. She felt a warm hand squeeze hers on the counter before she looked up.

"Randy."

She opened her mouth and shut it again, before she nodded.

"I and your dad are happy, Sean is a good person but you have been spending more time with Randy, are you now doubting your choice?"

She shook her head, "I am not, I mean I have dated Sean for some years now and also I know him. We know his family and we move in the same circle."

Her mother took a bite of the toast before she thoughtfully looked at her and remarked, "In all your reasoning I failed to hear the most important thing of all."

Elsie looked at her in confusion and Aggy smiled slightly, "Love. You didn't mention that you love Sean."

"That's rather obvious mom or I wouldn't be getting married to him after all."

"Ah huh" she nodded her head and got up from the stool.

Ethan had come in and greeted them.

"Coffee or tea" her mother asked her dad. "Tea love" he replied before settling down on the stool his wife had vacated from and turning to Elsie.

"How is my princess doing? You must have slept late yesterday trying to think about your fairytale wedding."

She shook her head in denial, "I rather slept early yesterday" she replied and continued drinking her coffee.

"So how does Randy feel about this?" her step dad asked to her shock. Not him also. Yesterday he had been teary eyed with her mother and now this. Did they intend to confuse her also?

"Randy as a good friend, congratulated me." Slamming the cup on the counter after draining the contents from it, she got up. "I should get going" and retreated as fast as she could before her dad could ask her more questions.

Ethan's brow had risen in question at his wife after Elsie walked away, "What was that all about? Isn't Randy just a friend, I didn't expect her to react like that."

She shrugged her shoulders and handed him the plate. "I think she might be interested in Randy more than what meets the eye."

"Oooh and when did that happen?"

"I don't know love." She settled next to her husband and took a sip of coffee. She suspected what Elsie might be going through, since at one time she had been silly and echoed the same sentiments. Ethan on the other hand was the one who stopped her from doing that. She sighed and said, "I think Elsie has been trying to fight the title of being Luc's daughter and in trying to rub it off completely she might be lying to her own heart. She might think that after dating a person for some years and telling them she is not in love with them is more of Luc's style, who changed ladies like dresses and she doesn't want that."

"She is an intelligent girl, she will figure it out" Ethan said and spun her bar stool to face him before leaning in and kissing her. Responding to his questing tongue by deepening the kiss and wrapping her arms around his neck, she giggled like a school girl when she felt his warm hands inside her t-shirt on her back. She was still in awe at how he could look at her with desire in his eyes, not at all waning in that regard.

Lately she had noticed a few grey strands in her hair and Ethan had been loving even more telling her that as she aged she became more beautiful.

"The children are not yet up, it's a Saturday remember" he whispered in her ear and the warmth of his breath coursed through her body sending a shiver down her spine. Cradling his face and kissing him, she chuckled, "I know, shall we."

She squealed as he swiftly picked her up and strode off to their room.

Chapter Eight

ELSIE WAS muttering under her breath as she drove the car to school. She wasn't going to spend her Saturday mulling over what her parents had said. Randy didn't care or he would have knocked on the front door early in the morning and demanded she get married to him.

What era was she in where that happened anywhere? In real life they were no knights in shining armor. Off course she had witnessed her mother and friends have dreamlike, fairytale weddings and marriages but those ones lived in another generation where the men were still chivalrous. Their generation on the other hand was more of a hit and run kind of people. They slept together after having met of social media and did not take the time to really really know each other.

She wondered if Sean really knew her. Now that was a bad thought even to her thinking, it wasn't fair. Sean made time for her when he could.

Before she even knew it, she realized when it was too late and she had stopped the car that she had gone to Randy's place.

His nana came out having heard the car. She groaned and slumped her head on the steering wheel before straightening up, removing her seat belt and getting out of the car.

"Nana, I missed you and thought of dropping by to see you" she said as she walked up to her and gave her a hug.

"You know you are always welcome here Elsie. Come in love and you eat my chocolate chip cookies you look mighty thin."

Giggling at that, she followed the old woman into the house.

"Where are Lilly and Raff" she asked after settling down on the kitchen chair. Nana had been baking and the kitchen smelled wonderful, of vanilla, chocolate and cinnamon.

"They went for a school trip. They will be coming back tomorrow."

"And Randy?"

The grandmother shrugged her shoulders before handing her a glass of warm milk, "You know that boy works so much, he left early for the garage."

Elsie nodded her head and received the small plate that nana handed to her. She just couldn't resist her homemade chocolate chip cookies.

"So when are you going to find a woman for him?"

Choking on her milk, she let out a fit of coughs and placed the glass on the table as the old woman reached out to pat her back with a smile that would have reviled any model. The old woman is relentless; she thought and received a napkin to wipe her mouth.

"I am on it. Told Randy yesterday we had to change his appearance first. Have you seen his latest beard look, like a cave man?"

Nana giggled with glee at that as Elsie joined in.

"Hand me that cellophane paper dear" nana said. "I think these have cooled enough to be packaged" she said motioning to the cookies on the cooling rack.

Elsie went on to place the cookies in packets of six and threes before closing them. They worked in that manner, chatting as nana reminisced over her youth. She was shocked that so much time had passed when she heard Randy's voice.

"Afternoon nan, came to take a quick shower before going to my next job. Hey Elsie," he nodded at both of them before he continued on to his bedroom.

Elsie had nearly drooled, even with a bit of grease here and there on the work suit he was a sight to behold.

"Okay, pack these up in the boxes and put them in Randy's car. He will drop them at Mandy's kiosk so she sells them for me." Elsie nodded and watched Nana leave the room before she took the empty small boxes and put the now packaged cookies in them. She took them to the taxi, sighing out of relief when the boot opened before she stowed the boxes and went for more. After she was done she sat back in the kitchen and drained the remaining milk that was now cold before looking for nana.

Since she hadn't seen her in the living room, she wondered where nana must have disappeared to. Glancing at the watch on the wall, she knew Randy would have been done with the shower. They needed to talk. Nana hadn't minded her being in Randy's room at all since at times she had done her maths studies over at the place; her requirement was that the door was meant to be open all the time. They might have said they were the best of friends and Elsie had a boyfriend yet she didn't trust two growing children taking such a risk.

Taping lightly on the door, she didn't wait for an answer but got in, and gasped when she noticed Randy's abs before they were covered by the polo shirt he had been donning on.

He was wearing blue torn jeans and the black polo shirt was tightly stretched over his body, showing off his muscle. "Elsie what are you looking for, I could have been naked?" a raised brow speared her heart and had her panting before she shut the door tightly.

"We have to talk."

Randy was moving around the room still getting ready as he got a hair brush and brushed his short hair. "Can't it wait until another time, I have to rush."

"No it can't" she shook her head and steadily moved towards him.

"What's going on, you seem to be pissed at me."

"What makes you think that?"

Well the fact that he was frowning at her made her think that. He turned back and took a bottle of his cologne before spraying under his armpits and around his abs, having raised the shirt to do so. Elsie gulped. This was torture on its own and Randy appeared to be oblivious.

"Talk" Randy glanced at her through the mirror. She had settled at the edge of the bed and was looking at him as if he was an alien of some sort. Taking in the short jumpsuit, he almost went and knelt down next to her and confessed his love, except his eyes locked on something on her finger, the ring. That made his frown deepen. Seeing she wasn't happy but rather seemed sad, he sighed and checked if all was in place before he turned and picked up her hands. "It's pretty and I can imagine very expensive"

"Wha-a-at-t" Elsie asked confused at what he was talking about. "The ring. Will Sean be comfortable in knowing that his fiancée was in my room and it's a habit she has?"

He dropped her hand and the bed dipped as he sat back to wear his socks and shoes.

"About this," she nervously chuckled, "It took me by surprise. I wasn't expecting it. We had planned to get married when I was done with school but Sean felt that he couldn't wait any longer." "Okay.."

Is that all he could say. What was wrong with Randy? There he was now standing up as if her decision didn't matter to him, not even a bit.

"I am sorry" she whispered and stood up to leave the room only for him to grab her hand and turn her around to face him.

He was still frowning and she resisted the urge to kiss it away.

"What are you sorry for Elsie; we are nothing more than good friends." The way he said it, so dismissively while his face had shown another emotion, that he was mightily pissed. It wouldn't surprise her if he threw her out of his room and said worse things about her character and on how she had been leading him on before getting engaged instantly the moment her absentee boyfriend popped the question.

"I mean" she gulped at the broad chest near her and looked up braving the frown, "I don't want you to get a wrong impression of me."

"And what is that impression princess," he asked and changed his tone almost to a growl while she gulped a few breaths of air.

"That I am tease."

"Who said you were a tease," his brow furrowed before he leaned in and whispered, "do you know what a tease does Elsie, she dresses seductively, leads the person on with her cute plump lips that beckon for him to kiss her and then pushes him away as if he were nothing."

He had shifted his hold and had drawn her to him by her waist while he spoke.

Elsie's heart thudded at a fast pace as she looked intrigued at the many emotions passing on Randy's face. From being angry now she saw desire instead and intent as he lowered his head and Elsie shut her eyes before she felt a slight brush of his warm lips on her.

Finally the long awaited kiss. She trembled as he parted her lips with his tongue before sliding it in and invading her being. She trembled further and could feel her legs about to buckle at the intrusion and instantly opened up her mouth, relishing the kiss and tasting in the sweetness it offered.

She moaned and could feel her back partly press against the wall while she clung to him and her hands ran over his strong arms. The kiss went on for a long time and his hands were at work also as he cradled her butt, groaning in the process, swiftly picked her up and wrapped her legs around his waist.

He leaned in, pressing her against the wall before trailing his warms lips onto her neck and ear where he playfully nipped it making her squirm. This was wrong on all levels, she thought and at the fact that she was engaged to Sean and his engagement diamond ring sparkled and mocked her for being such a hussy and having her arms around Randy. Yet she couldn't resist the sensations that he was making her feel. It was as if she was feeling everything strongly and for the first time.

A deep dull ache had settled between her thighs. It had been so long since she last felt that and with Randy she knew she could lose it if she didn't stop. She didn't want to be that girl again, who was led by her body instead of thinking about the consequences, hell she wasn't that thirteen year old anymore.

What would Randy think about her if he knew that once upon a time she had experienced the thrills of lovemaking? No matter what her dad said, that she was good, she wasn't, she was a bad girl and Randy deserved better than her. Even Sean, except when she told him, he accepted her, history and all. Her hand slowly trailed to his cheek rubbing the prickly beard with her sensitive palm and they finally drew apart from the long kiss as Randy let her go. Her feet hit the ground while they both tried to catch their breath at what had just happened.

Elsie cleared her throat, she didn't want to look his way, suddenly feeling contrite over her actions before she whispered, "I should go" and walked away. Randy was about to stop her but thought much better and dropped his hand. After five minutes and he was thinking straight, having composed himself, he left the room and found his nana in the living room with a ball of wool and knitting pins.

"What did you do this time that had Elsie run out from here like she was being chased?"

She stared at him with a frown pasted on her face.

"Nothing," he answered with a bite in his voice. He could hear her scoff at the lie but wasn't ready to confront his demons. Off course he was mighty pissed off with her. She didn't think about him and the fact that she could give them a chance before she agreed to the proposal.

At the end she chose what she believed would give her what she wanted in life, stability.

He could do that, give her that though it wouldn't be the same like to what she was used to. And to think he had almost made a fool out of himself the day before and shown her that he was interested in her and not as a friend. Hell, she was right, she was a tease. She had been goading him on to seduce her at the same time instantly forgot about it when her knight produced the diamond ring. What did that make him at the end of the day?

One of the bleeps in her ten year old plan.

Rita had mentioned it before, that Elsie had a plan on what she wanted, including the qualities of the man she wanted to marry her. He had to be loaded, a hard worker, family man, believer and so on. He wasn't loaded yet he had for a second thought that she might be in love with a man like him, who would love her with his being and provide for her as he had been doing for his family. He wouldn't be able to buy her designer clothes and send her to exotic places but he knew he could make her happy.

Give her the home she never had but that he was blessed to have had with his parents before their passing. They had been happy and content; his father so in love with his wife and it could be seen even by their kids as they loved touching each other a lot, holding hands, taking long walks with the children to the beach, chasing them away while they had their candlelit dinners and laughter. There was always so much laughter in the house.

"Did she mention to you that she is getting married?"

His nana frowned before it changed into pity guessing what might have sent Elsie running. The way her grandson was scowling said it all. "What are you going to do about it?"

"Nothing, she made her choice she will have to live by it."

His grandmother sighed but didn't push.

"The cookies are already in your car; don't you want to eat something before you leave?"

He shook his head, "I will grab something on the way" he advised before he reached out to her and kissed her on the forehead. "You take care," she whispered while he straightened up, smiled sadly and walked out of the house.

ELSIE SQUEEZED HER legs together trying to stop the deep dull ache she was feeling in between her legs. Celibacy by all means was hard to muster, she thought and yet she had managed it. That had all been because she kept as far away from compromising situations as she possibly could. Sean wasn't the type to try to take liberties from her, he was far much of a gentleman and Randy was that too.

Yet now she was in danger of causing Randy to be something else. She stroked her lips with her manicured thumb, grazing the tender skin still reliving what had just happened. She had pulled her car on the side after she left Randy's house in a daze. Her phone rang and she answered it without checking the caller I.D.

Sean's deep voice resonated from the phone. "Hey love, am from talking to your parents we will be having dinner at seven at my family house, make sure you dress well like a soon to be wife," he advised.

"Thanks Sean. See you at seven then." There was a slight pause from Sean before his voice drifted through again, "I was thinking we could meet up before that. It has been long since we had some quality time together."

Elsie bit her tongue and stifled a sob. Sean sounded so happy while she was fighting against the confusion welling up in her. He wouldn't be with another woman, kiss her crazy like she had done with Randy and still expect to marry her. She thought on what Rita once told her, that she should give each man the chance to find a woman who would love them whole heartedly. She really was a tramp, she thought.

"Its fine Sean, where can we meet?"

He mentioned the spot before he hung up. Heaving a sigh after the call, she started the car and drove towards the place where she would meet him.

Chapter Nine

FOR THE next couple of weeks everything passed in a blur. She was busy with school, meeting up with Sean's family and preparing for the engagement party. Sean's young sister Serena was elated by the news while his mother as usual didn't reveal her emotions. Grace Compton was a hard person to please and acted like her son was beyond reach and above reproach. How couldn't she, since Sean was a good man and not at all like the Compton's who didn't value marriage but rather still remained the talk of the town because of their womanizing ways.

She didn't meet Randy in that time and he also appeared to not be interested in looking for her. They hadn't even spoken over the phone after the kissing incidence. She was afraid if she called he would not answer so she didn't put the effort. Besides Nana had mentioned that he barely came home, he had taken up another job at the station that meant his shifts were at night after he was done with his day job.

"So when will I see you dear?" Nana had asked over the phone.

"I am quite busy but soon," she had sadly answered back. They was no turning back. With the preparations in hand, she couldn't drop everything and announce to Sean that she loved Randy more. Theirs was a crazy sweet kind of love that made her want to scream at the top of lungs and leave everything behind. That she had rather prefer being a middle class woman, without the trust funds and the exotic trips as Randy would take her into those places in the comfort of their bedroom.

If the kiss was an indicator to the joy she might derive from sex, then she knew the actual did will be out of the world. Today was her engagement party and she was rather chiding herself over the fact that she wasn't happy but rather felt sad and wished someone would untangle the mess she had gotten herself into.

Nita, Wendy and Marylyn were back home from school and the house was even noisier than before. Rita had also come for the engagement party but she could swear that her best friend wasn't her usual chirpy self but looked rather forlorn as if she had lost her best friend. She wondered why but wasn't ready to deal with someone's issues when she on the other hand felt like she would abscond her party.

"Can I come in," Nita tapped on the door twice before she got into her room.

"Looking beautiful Elsie," she commented and settled down on the bed. "Thanks, I would give to have your body though." Elsie giggled and watched her young sister roll her eyes through the mirror. "So no more clubbing for you, who will I go with?"

"Wendy."

Nita grimaced, "Have you seen Wendy and the way she rolls her eyes at everything. For someone who wants to be a writer, she certainly knows how to deflate a person's happy aura," she motioned with her hands over her body and sat up properly when Wendy burst in and asked beneath her glasses, "Who deflates a person's aura."

"You see what I mean; she could have made a wonderful headmistress at our school. Let me get ready and rival the bride to be," she winked before she sauntered off from the room. Wendy hugged her and commented on her appearance before she left her also to get ready. Time was moving fast. She stared at herself in the mirror for one last time before she got up and went downstairs to wait for everyone else. She appeared to have finished first before everyone as the rest banged their doors in a rush, getting all set for the party. It was going to be a small affair with family and close friends. She was glad that all her uncles would be there and hoped that none of the family members would cause a scene. Drama appeared to be their norm.

Chapter Ten

AGGY WAS furiously eating the tidbits offered on the buffet while looking from one end of the room to the other.

"What is going on Aggy?" Sophie asked with a raised brow and was shocked when her friend grabbed a glass of champagne and gulped it down in one go. For one meant to be celebrating her daughter's engagement she was nervous.

"Whoah, relax" Sophie advised and took the other glass from her hand that she was about to chuck down also.

"Trouble is what is going on" Aggy whispered and ran her eyes to the other side of the hall again. Sophie followed her eyes to where they were focused and saw a tall young broad shouldered man dressed in a suit. His legs were partly parted while his hands were in both pockets and he was staring through hooded eyes at the couple ahead of him. Sophie looked at the young man again; his stance reminded her of Greg her husband and even Ethan and Dominic, she had seen that look before they did something scandalous and freaked out afterwards when they had done it, that look that boded more on ill than good.

"Who is that?"

"Trouble," Aggy answered and gasped when the young man strode to the couple.

"I should stop this." Before she could walk towards her daughter, Ethan grabbed her hand and also Greg had moved towards them.

"Don't intervene," he whispered in her ear while Greg appeared to be whispering something to his wife. "He will ruin her reputation," Aggy snapped back.

"No he won't, let the kids sort their mess out Aggs," he advised in his commanding voice. Everyone else around them seemed to be oblivious on a scandal that was about to happen. Sean's parents were beaming chatting with the guests while Marg rolled her eyes at something Dominic might have said. He was being a nuisance as usual without his wife around.

Aggy looked to where Elsie and Sean stood and sighed relieved that the fireworks were not about to blow up. That sad demeanor had been a dead giveaway that Elsie wasn't happy with Sean after all and now with Randy staring at her in that manner, she realized that the feelings were mutual; Randy was also in love with her daughter.

For a while she had thought it was a one sided kind of thing and hoped Elsie would be happy with Sean. She wasn't going to see that now.

What she had been dreading happened. Randy asked for a dance from Elsie and her fiancé nodded and watched them go to the dance floor.

"Randy what is going on," Elsie asked in confusion while Randy didn't reveal anything but rather took her hand and placed it on his shoulder. Elsie stared at him, God he looked handsome and seeing him without his beard, cleanly shaven and wearing a suit was proving to be making her senses reel from the shock. It had been a while. When she spotted him across the room she had thought that she was dreaming and her heart had leapt at the sight of him in a suit and looking like one ready to conquer the world.

"Give me a minute of your time and I will never ever bother you again." He twirled her around before she moved back into his arms. "It's not a good time Randy, you have been avoiding me for weeks and now you show up like this."

"I am sorry," he smiled and she nodded. He knew and she knew she couldn't resist him. Sean was dancing with Nita and the room was rather a bit crowded as people appeared to love to dance so they easily slipped out of it.

"Do you know you are so beautiful," Ethan asked Aggy and watched her giggle like a teen. "I could mistake you for being Elsie's sister than mother" he whispered before kissing her. He had managed to take her mind off her daughter. He scowled when he saw Elsie slip out after Randy, maybe his wife had been right, Elsie was still young to know what she wanted. Aggy wouldn't be too happy if she realized that she had gone, hopefully it was just for a minute and she would come back.

He twirled his wife around shrugging off his thoughts from his daughter, and concentrating on Aggy who was glowing. Love did that to people. He looked to his mates slowly dancing with their wives and Dominic who appeared to be lonely. Dominic suddenly smiled and he knew what had made him that way before he saw her, his beautiful wife Juliet had made it after all.

It was some minutes after Juliet arrived when they heard angry voices above their loud music and some guests peered through the windows and it dawned on Ethan that what his wife had been dreading must have taken place.

He looked to where Sean had been dancing with Nita and nearly swore before he pulled his wife and they went outside. Sean was getting into his car, Elsie trailing behind and Randy clutching her arm. He said something to her that made her flinch. He angrily answered the phone and Elsie made a dash for it when he was doing so to her car so she could follow Sean. For a second Randy looked dejected, he got into his car and drove away except to the opposite direction.

"What is going on?" Aggy asked. Grace, had come out first at hearing the commotion hence she turned to Aggy and angrily stated, "Your daughter broke my son's heart. He caught her making out with that boy. Do you know anything about it?"

She glared angrily at the couple as the other relatives joined them outside.

"Look Grace, let's not cause a scene, we can talk this out away from prying eyes," Aggy begged.

Grace scoffed, "I should have known, like mother like daughter,"

"Look here that's my wife you are talking about," Ethan angrily cut in.

The tension was palpable as the parents for the children who had run off from their engagement glared at each other. The only one who appeared not to be interested was Sean's father who was still in the hall chatting with his colleagues while outside, daggers from everyone's eyes were being thrown around.

Pastor Garret managed to intervene before things got out of hand and made some of the guests who had come out due to the fact that they liked gossip, return back into the hall while he was left with the parents. His cousin wasn't helping at all, the supposedly mature father Luc was chuckling and remarking, "Scandals never end in this family."

He glared at him and Luc stopped laughing but rolled his eyes instead before he followed the rest who had gone into the side room that was usually used as an office at the venue they had hired. Greg groaned and went back to the hall to apologize to the guests before dismissing them. Hopefully none of what had happened would find its way into another of the so called sensational papers.

⸺⊙⸺

"SEAN I CAN EXPLAIN," Elsie said trailing behind him and weeping. She hadn't wanted to hurt him like that and on their engagement to top it all. He was her friend above everything else and he needed her. She wasn't going to think about Randy's threat that if she left with Sean that would be the end of them. They will never be together again.

Sean abruptly stopped and whirled to face her before holding her by the shoulders.

"How do you explain that away Elsie" he angrily asked and she flinched. He let go of her and put his hands in the pockets of his trousers still glaring daggers at her.

"I swear it will never happen again" she choked out a sob and Sean scoffed. She was testing his patience as she usually did, this time what she had done couldn't be fixed. They were to be married for God's sake and he had caught her making out with someone else, who did that, just let it slide and moved on.

"I have been a fool, thinking you and Randy were nothing more than friends, for how long have you been in love".

Elsie looked away still teary eyed.

"How long Else" he bellowed and she flinched again before looking up to him.

"I have been in love with Randy for a while now."

He looked at her in disbelief, which meant when he asked she already knew that she was no longer interested but told him to relax, it was nothing.

"And what is this Elsie that we have" he motioned with his hands between the two of them. "Why didn't you mention that you couldn't be married to me because you were in love with someone else?"

"I was still confused Sean because I love you too?"

"Can you even hear yourself woman?"

He knew it looked like he was chiding his child instead of fiancée yet he couldn't control the anger churning inside of him. And to think he had felt guilty over being attracted to her friend when she was doing more than just chatting. She might have been sleeping with him for all he knew.

"What is it that he has, that I don't have, hmmm" he grabbed her pulling her by the waist and kissed her to inflict pain.

"Sean you are hurting me," Elsie wept and tried to wiggle from his grasp.

"Is it the sex that is good?" he still held her firmly and Elsie gasped.

"No Sean, please don't do this, you are not like this."

Finally she managed to get out of his arms and they stared at each other, one sad and tears running down her face, and the other with red rimmed eyes, seething with fury.

"Go to him," he spoke and turned away.

"I can't."

He whirled back to face her. "What is wrong with you? What do you want?"

"He told me to choose, if I followed you that is the end of us."

Sean raised his hands and dropped them in defeat. He moved close and heaved in a deep breath and out. Unclenching his hands that had been balled in a fist he asked, "Should I be happy that you chose me, should I be grateful. Tell me what I should feel. Are you a bloody martyr of some sort?"

He looked at her as she wept. He was hopeless when it came to women crying and would have preferred the fiery Elsie to this weepy one.

He sighed and pulled her in his arms. "Why can't you be with him, I am fine with it."

She looked up, "You know why."

He swore when she said that. She was settling because he knew her past that haunted her at times.

"Why didn't you tell him?"

"I was scared"

"So you figured out that since am a Compton and we don't stay faithful to our women will be even in the relationship. You with your past and me with my women on the side."

She gasped in shock at that statement, when said aloud it sounded so wrong.

"Elsie I told you that I don't want to be like the men in my family, but you want that right. A loveless marriage, and don't say you love me, you don't do what you just did to the person you love."

Since they were outside the house that his father had given to them as a gift, Elsie sat on the step and Sean followed suit.

"I am sorry Sean?"

He nodded.

"I am pathetic."

"We are a pathetic bunch," he said and she glanced at him, wondering what he meant.

"Will you be ok?" she asked him and he nodded.

"I am sure am not the first guy to be dumped at his engagement party," he chuckled. Her phone started ringing and she reached out for it. It was her mother, she was worried. "I am fine ma. I am with Sean right now."

His phone rang and he answered it while Elsie continued with hers. After he was done with the phone call, he stated, "I am not going home today. I don't know about you, but I am sleeping here for the night, not in any mood to answer some questions."

He stood up and unlocked the door to their house. So much for trying not to be like her scandalous family, she thought. She stood up and followed him into the house.

Chapter Eleven

RANDY PACED up and down the corridor of the hospital and savagely pulled at the constricting tie around his neck. He was angry with himself and also at the fact that he appeared to be too late. His nana had been on his case telling him to stop things before they went far, except he thought if Elsie was serious about him she would come back. She had created the whole mess and she had to clean it up.

The doctor opened the door to the ward and motioned for him to get in. "How is she?" he asked and looked at nana lying on the bed.

"She is fine; she just experienced a mild stroke. I will write out a prescription of drugs you will have to get from the dispensary for her. She will also have to come for physiotherapy for her hand to be worked on so that it functions the normal way it used to."

Randy nodded and the doctor smiled at him before she left the room.

"Nan, you gave Lilly and Raff a scare," he chided and the old woman chuckled.

While in the midst of talking to Elsie and a furious Sean who had walked away, Lilly had called and informed him that Nan fainted and they were failing to revive her, she was hysterical and he couldn't do anything apart from attending to his family first.

"What happened to your eye," Nan asked in a loud enough voice barely the woman who had almost gone to be with the Lord. The eye was red and slightly swollen. Randy laughed. "The young man can surely throw a punch" He answered.

"You should have dealt with this before the engagement party."

He scoffed and settled back next to her. "I wish I hadn't gone there," he wearily said.

"Why?"

"She chose him again. When push came to shove, she left me and chose him."

"Ooh Randy." His nana reached out to him with her functional hand. "Don't strain to move. I will let Lilly and Raff sleepover at Rita's place for today. I will come and see you in the morning. Don't die on me," he jested. "We still need you."

Nana laughed quietly, "I am strong my boy, once I get off this bed, you will regret ever thinking that I am weak."

He bent over and kissed her on the forehead before he left.

———◆———

ELSIE OPENED HER EYES and stretched on the bed. Sean had occupied the main bedroom last night while she took the guest bedroom. She had discarded her dress on the chair before dozing off. She looked like a wreck and she knew it. She leapt out of bed and attended to a need at hand and washed her hands and face afterwards, grimacing at the mascara that had run over her face the previous night.

Getting into the shower, she let the warm water sooth her and could hear a few sounds coming from the kitchen once she was done and wore her dress again. She should have listened to her mom, when she advised her to leave a change of clothes last week when the Senior Compton gifted them with the house.

They had joked a bit with Sean yesterday both claiming that his father was likely to take back the house, seeing they were not going to get married.

"Hey," Sean greeted when she got into the kitchen and placed their breakfast on the kitchen counter. He was dressed in a golf t-shirt and jeans to her utter shock. Sean Compton in jeans, that was a first, she thought.

"I am surely going to miss this house," he commented and she giggled.

"I immediately brought food and a few clothes that I had rather be caught wearing here and no other place after dad handed us the keys."

"Darling you should have mentioned and I would have done the same. Now look, I will have to go home and face the music this early."

Sean reached out to her hand and squeezed it. "Are you sure you are going to be fine though. I mean your prince charming dumped you. You dumped me for him and he dumped you because of me."

"Okay, okay, Mr. Topnotch lawyer, stop rubbing that fact in," she said in a drawl before she changed her voice to a lighter tone and asked "Are you fine with this though. You are not angry that I dragged you along all this while." He rolled his eyes as she spoke.

"I am relieved that I dodged a bullet."

She huffed and punched his arm. "If I knew a thing or two, I could swear you must be having a woman on the side, that's why you have an upbeat attitude about this whole thing." His jaw dropped and he shut it without uttering a word. Sean speechless, that was a first, she was right after all. He also had been hiding some skeletons in his closet.

"Well I hope whoever the woman is, makes you miserable like hell. I can't believe you had been about to make me the scapegoat."

Sean laughed and answered, "Let's go. The sooner we deal with our problems the better. Advice to the wise girl, you indeed are the forward one. Smooching up a lover and almost stripping each other's clothes off while you were engaged to someone else. Brr, I am shocked Elsie Cooper, who taught you to be that way."

Elsie huffed and stood up from the chair before clearing up their breakfast dishes and they walked out of their house.

"Come here you, for old times' sake; let me hug away your worries. I could have been doing this for you for life," Sean stated and she giggled at that before she went into his arms once they were outside and had locked the door to the house.

"If I need rescuing, I will call you." Sean whispered before he straightened up, smiled, got into his car and drove off. After he had left and she walked to her car a bit further away, she decided to finally switch on her phone and the messages from relatives and friends started trickling in.

One voice message, she wondered who it was and listened to it. Lilly was hysterical and couldn't get hold of Randy. Oh God, Nan, she thought and rushed to the car before she drove to the Medical Centre where she knew nan would be, since it wasn't the first time she had fainted for a long time like that. She was present when Nan once collapsed before.

RANDY SWORE UNDER HIS breath when he saw Elsie and Sean in a passionate embrace outside the house. Nita had been kind enough to inform him that Elsie hadn't gone home the previous night and she was at her place that her father in law had gifted her with. He knew the neighborhood since it was made up of new houses and only a few people occupied it. It was a quiet and good neighborhood for starting a family in. The residential stands were rather pricey and he guessed this was another ploy used by the influential and rich to segregate themselves from the rest. The more they made money, the more private they became with their lives.

Slowly passing the oblivious couple as Sean whispered something to Elsie, he drove on to the hospital. That was the last straw and he should forget about ever being with Elsie. She didn't seem like one ready to be with him. The fact that she still wore the same dress she had on yesterday told him the rest of what he needed to know. Her relationship with Sean ran deeper than she had said and she had spent the night with him while he worried over Nan her supposedly best friend.

ELSIE BURST INTO THE ward and momentarily halted when she noticed Randy standing over his granny. "Nan, how are you feeling?" She rushed to her and gave her a hug.

"I am fine, like I keep on tell Randy also. I can't wait to get up from this bed." She chuckled while she sat up. Elsie helped her by plumping a few pillows behind her. She looked over to Randy and noticed the disgust he had on his face and cringed.

"Nan, I have to go to work, I will see you in the evening." He said, kissed her on the forehead before he walked away without a backward glance to his former friend and almost girlfriend. Elsie wanted to rush to him but was stayed from doing so by Nan who clutched at her arm using her still functional right hand.

"He needs time love," she whispered. Elsie slumped in defeat on the seat next to the bed.

"I fear I have lost him for good this time." Nana shook her head. "Don't you think its time you opened up a bit to him."

"No Nan, I can't, didn't you see the disgust he has for me. If I am to tell him, he will seize even from being my friend." She had abruptly stood up and was pacing in the ward when Nan suggested that. "Come here," Nan motioned and she went back to settle next to her. "Elsie, Elsie, when will you stop concluding on how a person will react before you tell them. So will you get married to Sean because he accepted that secret about you and forgo being with the one that you truly love."

"Why do I have to mention it anyway Nan, I mean I can have a happy relationship without digging my past." Nan tsk, tsked in disappointment. "It's because what happened then is part of you and makes you who you are Elsie. You also see the hand of God at work, not by concealing but by exposing. I mean the apostle Paul at a later stage once said I am the worst of sinners. He had seen something more to make him say that, the grace of God over his life. When you look at your past see it as that the past and focus on the grace and the power of

God to have restored you into something much stronger than what you were."

"I don't think I can do this."

Nana sighed and motioned for her to hug her. "It is well," she said and lay back on the bed. "So what did you decide with Sean."

"It's over. The man had the audacity to happily tell me he dodged a bullet."

Nana cackled with glee at Elsie's shocked face. "Sean is a good man, am sure he will find a girl worthy of him soon enough."

Elsie huffed, "Are you saying I wasn't good enough." Nan chuckled at her offended expression. "Just go home, change your clothes those are definitely not for day time and stop being a nuisance." She jested and Elsie hugged her again before she left. She already knew that the whole clan would be waiting for her at home and they needed answers. God help me, she sent the silent prayer looking heavenward before she drove off from the hospital.

Chapter Twelve

IT WAS two weeks after her broken engagement and everything seemed to finally have settled down a bit. As she had guessed, after her visit with nana she found the whole family waiting for her at home and demanding for answers over her untoward behavior. She rolled her eyes at that word that her favorite uncle Greg had used and her father Luc and Ethan had chuckled at it, not helping matters.

She almost retorted back that, it was their scandalous history that made her that way. Each one of them had exhibited an untoward behavior including the scowling Uncle Greg who wanted answers while her fathers couldn't stop sniggering at her expense.

Who would wish for advisors if her fathers happened to be the worst in sorting out her problems? Luc had the audacity to state that she was Ethan's problem, while Ethan scowled and said it was Luc's blood coursing through her body that was the problem. Only uncle Garret appeared to be the reasonable one.

She was grounded for three days. Imagine that, a twenty year old, independent lady being treated in the same manner like her twin sisters, that's when she had really wished she stayed far away from home.

She took the punishment at its stride and her siblings entertained her. Wendy interviewed her and was contemplating writing a story about her love affairs while the rest of the sisters who understood things pertaining to dating giggled at her expense.

"A scandalous engagement, that's the title of my play," Wendy stated with flourish while Elsie grimaced.

"One day you will find yourself in such a situation, don't forget you are also a Cooper," she retorted and her sister rolled her eyes. "Never, I am not you, maybe Nita is likely to fall into that trend but I refuse to follow tradition" Wendy proudly declared and winked at her.

Nita protested also at that suggestion, "Wendy you are seventeen and already a huge flirt. Elsie even looks like a saint compared to you." Wendy huffed and walked out of the room with her book where she had been scribbling some points on.

"You shouldn't say that love." Elsie said to Nita amidst giggles. "Huh, don't let those glasses fool you, Wendy is the worst and I stand on that" Nita declared before she informed her she was going out. As usual she was rubbing it in that Elsie wasn't meant to venture out of the house for three days until things settled down.

She decided to extend her days and finally two weeks later she was ready to venture out into the real world. Nan had called; she was out of hospital and wanted to meet with her. After getting ready, she walked down the stairs and found everyone having breakfast.

"Back from exile I see," her step dad said with a raised brow while her mother greeted her and she sat down for coffee. "So what is the first thing you want do?" her mother asked.

"I am going to visit Nan." Her mother clutched her head before she waved her hands in defeat. "You are a hopeless case," she said and Elsie giggled since they was humor in her eyes.

"I need to marry her off fast, she is just trouble you know that. I should talk to Randy to take her quickly, they isn't a need for him to pay the bride price. He will have her free of charge," her step dad said and she gaped her mouth.

She didn't think she was that troublesome. She gulped down the coffee quickly before they all ganged up and got on her case again. "I can't believe they have been so many detours in that ten year plan." Her mother added staring at her husband while Elsie rolled her eyes. The sooner she got out of there, the better she thought and walked out of the room.

"NAN!" SHE CALLED OUT but there was no answer. Nan had mentioned that she will be home and now she had come to an empty house. She could hear the water in the shower fading away and thought maybe it was Nan who was done with her bath, so she settled down on the couch and waited. The door at the back had been opened widely and she wondered were Raff and Lilly where. Maybe at Rita's, she would check them up later on.

She suddenly felt nervous and wondered if she would meet Randy. From the way his grandmother had been protective over him, she knew it was unlikely that Nan would call her whilst he was around.

"Nan, I will see you in the evening" Randy said getting into the living room and stopped when he saw her.

"Where is nan?"

She shrugged her shoulders. "I don't know; thought it was her taking the shower, found the back door wide open."

He nodded and scowled before he remarked, "Please pass the message when she comes back. She should be ready by seven pm for our date."

"Is that it Randy, you are not going to talk to me."

He had turned and was now leaving. He turned around and angrily asked, "What is there to talk about Elsie. You made your choice. Why are you here anyway, have you come to gloat?"

She was outraged at what he was saying and stood up. Of all people meant to know her, she never thought he would misunderstand her that much.

"That is not fair Randy. I thought in these two weeks you would have calmed down. I see there isn't any hope to reason with you. I should be the one leaving; you can deliver your message to your granny yourself."

She brushed past him and he caught her arm, whirling her around. "Whoa princess, what's the rush? Why are you leaving, let's talk. You wanted to talk right, let's talk."

He folded his arms over his chest and glared at her, blocking also her path to the door.

"Never mind, let me pass, I should go."

"You see, you have nothing to say after all. Go Elsie, runaway like you usually do. I no longer care at all. You can live your life the way you deem fit and count me as nothing else apart from a lapse of judgment."

He angrily turned around to leave. Elsie knew if she didn't speak now she would lose Randy for good. Anyway by the way he had been looking at her, she had lost him already. What would revealing her past do, apart from putting the final nail to the coffin?

"Randy I terminated a pregnancy when I was just thirteen years old" she blurted out. He had reached the door, but turned back to face her, shock evident on his face.

"I feel ashamed okay. Is that what you want to know," she frantically said and wrapped her arms protectively around herself like a shield.

It was now or never. Seeing Randy hadn't walked out but was now waiting for her to talk prompted her to hesitatingly continue. "At thirteen, I had done things not even a normal teenager or adult would. I wanted to be loved and sort validation from men. I told myself it didn't matter all could be handled with just the rubber, it was impersonal. I dated men almost my father's age and slept with some of them. Justin was the only teen I dated. We were one of a kind. He introduced me to the night clubs and the alcohol, the fake IDs and the drugs. One day I came home and heard sounds from my parents' room. Mom had left with my siblings for the farm and I had refused to join them and so I remained with dad. I went over to the room and opened the door. There was my dad with another woman. I quickly shut the door but he followed a few minutes later, handed me his visa card and told me to buy something pretty for myself. He needed me to take myself away from the house for a few hours. I have always known that my mom hid a lot of things about my dad but still I never knew that it had come to that extent that he brought the women home." She shrugged her shoulders and paced the room. "I was confused, hurting and my father didn't love me the way a father was meant to. Who does that, bribes their daughter to be away from home so he could have his time with other women. I tried to get hold of Justin; his number was not reachable so I went over to his place. He had a couple of friends made up of boys and girls mostly Justin's age, seniors at the school we attended. I and another girl were the only ones in our early teens. They were having a party."

Randy stopped her from pacing in the room by holding her shoulders. She could see the compassion in his eyes but doubted it would be there for long. "It wasn't an ordinary party of youngsters just having fun, with toys and water guns." She flatly spoke, devoid of emotion.

"It was an orgy; I drank like the rest of them and didn't care what happened to me. They were four senior boys, Justin included. Oh God, I am so disgusted." She shifted away from his arms and went to sit on the couch. "I was back at school when I found out I was pregnant and I didn't know who the father was." Her voice cracked.

"I was young, confused with no one to talk to. They are some senior girls that I knew who were well versed, so they helped me by recommending a place where I could take care of it. I came back home over the weekend and went to the place. I got rid of it, went and partied till dawn afterwards. I just wanted to forget, not to feel anything and alcohol had a numbing effect to do just that. It was on our way when we were returning home that we had the accident. None got hurt apart from a few scratches sustained but the car was beyond repair. It was a miracle that we even got out of there."

She stood up again and started pacing around the living room and rubbing her arms while Randy remained at the same spot she had left him. This was the first time in a long while since she had spoken about it. At the moment she didn't want to look at Randy and see the disgust in his eyes. Heaving a sigh, she continued, "That's how mom and Ethan found out everything. I guess that accident also made me to take introspection of my life. Would an older version of me be proud of the choices I had made? I was disgusted with myself Randy and I thought I didn't deserve to live. I was promiscuous and I thought myself to be weird compared to the rest of the teens my age but I remember pastor G saying I could start over, on a new slate. That God was a God of many chances and He never forsook me even when I was doing all those things, that it was His grace that had made me realize my mistakes and want to change. That's how I took a vow to remain chaste until I got married. You see," she shrugged her shoulders as the tears slid down her face.

"I am not the princess that you mistake me to be. I have a dark past. My mother sent me to a public school so I could get a dose of reality and also so she could keep an eye out on me. No matter how hard I try to shake off that past, it haunts me. I don't deserve anything good because of what I am and I fear that I might not even be faithful to you or any man who will come into my life."

"Ooh princess", Randy crooned and reached out to her before he engulfed her in a warm hug.

"Why didn't you tell me before," he asked.

"I was scared; I didn't want you to see me in that light. When I did tell Sean, he accepted me but it was as if something had shifted in our relationship. I didn't want that same thing to happen to you. For you to stay in the relationship because somehow you felt obligated but was no longer interested in me. On the other hand I couldn't tell Sean that it was better we broke it off when I realized you liked me too. Sean had stood by me and accepted me. It wouldn't be fair to him. I am sorry for being this way Randy."

Randy hugged her again and could feel her sobs shake her body as she wept. Abuse is what happened to her. He could very much imagine her seeking attention and trying to make up for the short comings she thought she had, that's why her father could treat her and her mother like that. Except the men never saw that weakness but used her to satisfy their own needs, just like the senior boys. All she wanted was to be loved. He hugged her and rubbed her arms. His sweet Elsie, he thought, so vulnerable and brave at the same time.

Elsie appeared to have exchanged one fear for another. Love covered a multitude of sins but in Elsie's case she appeared to have partly accepted that. She critically weighed everything against her past and thought no one would ever see the change and accept her the way she was now. She was afraid to feel, she was afraid to give herself whole heartedly and hence felt that she was more like her father if she failed to commit to anything.

He also knew that sex was a good thing in its proper context, marriage since it was God's gift and a person had to be at a certain age, mature in every way to engage in that. What did a thirteen old girl know?

He now understood why she had run off that day in his room and why she was quick in agreeing to get married to Sean after he told her he would seduce her in jest. She had been scared that she would revert to her former destructive self.

"It's okay," he whispered and pulled her to the couch before he settled down next to her. Wiping her eyes with the pad of his thumb, he softly remarked, "You don't look good when you cry."

She snorted outraged and he smiled.

"Only a few people know and I even told Rita on our last sleepover night before she went to varsity. I told her if she didn't want to be my friend anymore I would understand and she was like, girl you crazy."

Randy chuckled, that was Rita for sure.

"You are crazy indeed to have thought that love. That is your past and it should remain there." She sighed at that statement as it reminded her on what her uncle Garret would usually say.

Randy wrapped his arms around her and kissed her on the forehead. "I love you Elsie and after hearing this from you, even more. You are a brave woman."

She was shocked to hear that from him and he chuckled at the disbelief written on her face.

"You are the kindest and most loving young woman that I have ever met" he said.

"Do you know why nana likes you?"

Elsie shook her head since she didn't know where Randy was going with the conversation.

"She usually says, Elsie knows life, she knows pain and such a person can be understanding to ones weaknesses."

She giggled and asked, "What do you say to that?"

Crossing his hands over his chest and staring at her beneath the lashes, he grumbled, "Nan are you really talking about Elsie, that twittering silly girl."

Elsie pinched Randy on that note and he chuckled. "The old woman is right and I guess I was wrong and the fact that I took long in realizing what a mature young woman you are. It takes guts you know, to make up one's mind and live up to it, and you Elsie have done it."

Seeing the love in Randy's eyes and mirth instead of what she had expected, touched her at the core and another set of tears fell down her eyes. She really didn't deserve him, yet looking at him told her all she needed to know. He was here to stay. Randy tilted her chin up so their eyes were level with each other.

"Don't you think it's time we settled down and nana got the chance to meet her great grandchildren?"

She gasped and clasped his hand that still held her face as Randy knew instantly what she had been thinking. That he would not want her after the confession. No one was perfect after all. The fact that she was able to move on and not sleep around after her misdeeds showed her character to be exactly what he had thought. She was a committed, faithful person and would stand by her promises, even if she thought herself to be the opposite.

"I should add daft to my list of qualities about you" he remarked with a raised brow before he kissed her and didn't let her protest.

Epilogue

Two months later.

"DO YOU think she is going to run?" Nita asked with a smirk and Dustin, Rita's step brother poked her with his elbow. "That's your sister you are talking about."

"Well she does have a knack at drama, that's why I asked" she giggled and sat back to listen to the vows being made.

So far the engagement party two weeks back had been a success, she had even spotted Sean among the guests before he disappeared. He should be grateful he had dodged a bullet than be leg shackled with her sister. She was a drama queen and needed someone who could be firm like Randy.

Looking around the church, everyone was happy. Randy's Nan was beaming at the couple as if it was her wedding. Agatha was sniffling with a hanky over her mouth.

"Ooh mom" she thought and resisted the urge to roll her eyes, from the expressions coming from the men, her two dads, Luc and Ethan they seemed like they might faint any moment since they were holding their breaths, ready to saunter to the door and manhandle whichever man might show up and try to ruin Elsie again. One was enough and she appeared to love him dearly.

When the minister pronounced the couple as husband and wife, a round of applause reverberated in the whole church and she finally saw her dads smile.

Nita giggled and hoped she out of all the Cooper girls would be scandal free. First it had been her mother getting hitched to Ethan after having thought he was marrying someone else, an embarrassing scene of course, then it was Elsie with her botched up engagement party.

Already she could see Wendy was a big flirt and guessed her young sister would get married before her.

Drama, drama, drama is all that her family was good at.

She stood up and walked behind the happy couple. Ooh they were so in love they made her want to throw up in her mouth.

A cute guy smiled at her and she scowled, what did he think, that bridesmaids were easy.

Tilting her head up, she joined in the rest of the family and her beaming sister and new brother in law who were receiving best wishes from their guests.

Finally one problem down, six more other problems left, her sisters and young brother were yet to grow up and also venture into the tumultuous world of love, ooh yes and that included her.

Next In This Series

Marrying a Compton

Rita Duncan is horrified at finding out that she will be a mother before she is done with fulfilling her dream. What worsens the situation is the fact that the father of her unborn child is Sean Compton, her best friend's ex-fiancé. She can't remember their night together apart from the five hundred dollars; he considerately left on her bedside as proof of what he really thought about her.

With her nicely planned out life, what is a girl to do apart from get rid of the problem and live happily ever after, except she is scared and she decides to look for help from her best friend who would definitely be pissed off once she finds out about her betrayal. Nevertheless she is in desperate need of her help so she has clarity on what to do next.

Sean Compton is furious of having to chase after a woman who appears to employ every avoidance tactic she can think up. He wants to explain something to her but the ever evasive Rita will not let him. Finally he gives up and right on cue, the solution to his problem comes in the form of his ex-fiancée who drops a bombshell on him. Will he do the right thing or make the evasive Rita finally pay?

All Books By Yvonne Sibanda

<u>Family Matters Series</u>
The Inconvenient Marriage
Finding a husband for Cissy
A Risky Venture
<u>Perfect Gentleman Series</u>
The Perfect Gentleman
The Designer's Wicked Intentions
<u>Next Generation Series</u>
Sweet Crazy Love
Loving a Compton – Coming Soon

About Yvonne Sibanda

Yvonne Sibanda is a writer and author who loves a good story with a happy ending, hence adds her Christian values to her books. She has been a lifelong writer and began creating worlds and characters in the fourth grade. She lives and works out of her home in a small mining town of Hwange, Zimbabwe.

Where To Find Yvonne

Facebook https://www.facebook.com/vovosibbs/

Once in a while I drop a cover image of my latest books I am working on and also an update for my books that will be out. If they are any promotions running on some of the sites where I publish my books, I also drop in the information and link so you can easily use those to your advantage.

Thank you again for your support and for those who continue helping me in this journey. To God the Father, Son and the Holy Spirit, may your name be forever glorified. Amen.